PROJECT BLOODBORN

BOOK 2

WOLF SPIRIT

CRAIG ZERF

Anglo-American Press

As always – to my wife, Polly and my son, Axel. You chase the shadows from my soul.

The sun watches what I do, but the moon knows all my secrets.
J.M. Wonderland

TABLE OF CONTENTS

PROLOGUE

It had been over a week since Brenner had left the bayou. He had headed vaguely south, toward Texas, cruising slowly, taking in the scenery. Stopping early and sleeping late. Recovering.

But now it was a little under twenty-four hours until the full moon, so he was heading for less populated parts. Looking for a place he could chain himself up for the first night of the full moon. To stop him hurting innocent people during the change.

He had just stopped for gas and a soda when his satellite phone rang. He grabbed it from his saddlebag and hit the receive button.

'Griff,' he greeted. 'Waasuuup?'

'Listen, Brenner,' answered Griff. 'I don't have much time. I have swallowed a tracking device. It should transmit for the next twenty-four hours or so. My coordinates will show up on your phone. Shit, they're here,' he whispered. 'Look, I gotta go. Help me Brenner, please. You need to come as soon as, before they kill me.'

There was the sound of breaking glass. Then a gunshot.

Then, silence.

Brenner had twenty-four hours to find Griff.

And it was almost exactly twenty-four hours until the full moon.

Shit!

He checked the coordinates on his phone, jumped onto his Harley, gunned the engine, and took off.

1

The room was dark. Not pitch black. There was just enough light for Griff to make out the approximate size of the place as well as the fact there were at least another ten people there with him.

Like him they appeared to be shackled to the floor. A length of steel chain ran from a cuff on his right wrist, through a U-bolt in the floor to a corresponding cuff on his left wrist. There was enough play for him to sit or lay, but not to stand.

Griff had no idea how long he had been there. He remembered them coming for him. The phone call to Brenner. The fight. Them trashing his Winnebago. Tearing the hard drives from his computers, picking up his laptop, grabbing all the paperwork they could find.

He smiled to himself. Amateurs. They would find nothing on the hard drives. He had followed the protocol of the ultra-paranoid hacker and hit the red button as soon as they had shown up. Not only had that scrubbed the drives clean but it had also implanted a virus of his own making onto them, thereby ensuring anyone who tried to read them would suffer the consequences. Using the "I Love You" virus and blending it with the "Code Red" virus, Griff had written a new virus he called the "Dear John". As soon as they attempted to open his hard drives the "Dear John" would penetrate their systems and start to reproduce itself at an exponential rate until it had eaten up all the systems resources. Finally, it would display a message that read. "I'm so sorry, John. It's not you, it's me".

Griff was under no illusions the virus would result in the end of things. Quite the contrary. He knew, as soon as they had been attacked, they would come and find him and attempt to get info from him the old-fashioned way.

But that was later. He could hear the people around him moaning. Some coughed, some whimpered. A few, like him, remained silent. He could smell urine. So he could deduce they had been chained up long enough for people to start to lose control of their bladders. But it still didn't give him much of a time frame.

He knew he had been knocked unconscious during the take down but it had only been for a short time. Then they had drugged him. He had felt the needle in his arm, he had fought unsuccessfully against the soporific feeling, then he had woken here, in chains. With a hangover rivaling the very worst he had ever had before.

A door opened and flooded the room with light. People gasped and a few let out desultory shouts. Cries for attention, demands for explanations. They were ignored as three men walked straight toward Griff. They hauled the old man to his feet, unlocked his shackles, and dragged him from the room, closing and locking the door behind him.

The sun blasted his eyes as he exited. Mountains in the distance. Scrubland. Almost desert. Fences. Clapboard bungalows laid out in rows like some sort of military camp. Or prison. Griff stumbled and they pulled his chains tight, slapping him on the back of the head as they did so.

They crossed what seemed like a parade ground then through a doorway into one of the basic buildings. Along a corridor and into a bare room with three chairs and a wooden table.

There they slammed him into one of the chairs, pulled the chain behind his back and shackled him. The restraints were tight enough to prevent him from moving.

Sitting on the edge of the table was a man Griff immediately picked out as a leader. The three men who had dragged him in showed obvious signs of deference to the leader in both their body language and attitude.

He was short, slightly overweight, and wore a charcoal suit, red necktie, and black brogues. Shiny pink face. A large square cut diamond sparkled on his pinky finger, bringing attention to his soft manicured hands. But his eyes were his most arresting feature. Deep brown with ovoid pupils, they protruded slightly from their sockets. Almost as if he had just been choked. And the whites of his eyes showed all around the iris, giving him a fervent maniacal demeanor.

The eyes of a prophet.

He stared at Griff for a while. Silent. His eyes boring into his very soul. Then he spoke.

'They call me, The Pastor,' he said. 'And you would be, Reece Griffin. Sergeant. Army Ranger, Vietnam. Two silver stars, four purple hearts.' He stood and approached Griff, hands behind his back. He stopped two steps away and nodded. 'Thank you for your service.'

'Yeah,' said Griff. 'And fuck you very much, Pastor. What the hell am I doing here?'

The Pastor raised an eyebrow then made a small gesture with his head. A barely discernable tilt. One of the men who had dragged Griff in, walked over and punched the old veteran in the nose. Griff heard it break. A sound akin to a boot stepping on gravel. He felt the blood flow, warm and sticky, into his moustache and beard. He could taste the iron flavor in the back of his throat.

'You see, Mister Griffin,' continued the man in the suit. 'We know who you were, now we just need to know who you are at this moment in time. Are you simply some washed up Vietnam vet with PTSD or are you working for someone? And, if you are on someone's payroll, who?'

The man stood and waited in silence for a while. Eventually Griff spoke. 'I'm sorry, was that a question?'

The man nodded. 'Who do you work for? Why were you looking into our business? How much do you know?'

Griff thought for a few seconds. What he didn't want to tell the man was the truth. He didn't work for anyone. He was looking into their business due to a random search while looking for something else and it had led to them. And, finally, he knew next to nothing about them aside from the fact that only hours after he had started to look into them, people had tracked him down and kidnapped him. The reason Griff was loath to divulge this info was because he knew as long as they suspected he worked for some outside agency and they thought he knew more than he did, then they would have to keep him alive to get the information out of him.

The moment they knew he was an ignorant old man who worked alone and knew nothing … well, then he would have definitely outlived his usefulness and could look forward to little else than a shallow grave in the middle of nowhere. A fate he would like to avoid if at all possible.

Of course, there was a downside. He knew they would start putting some serious pressure on him to get the info out of him. And that meant his broken nose was the least of his worries. Worse was to come, of that he was certain.

However, he also knew Brenner was coming. So it was only a matter of time. And no matter how hard these boys thought they were, Griff didn't sweat them. He had been captured by the VC once while in Cambodia and had suffered in one of their camps for six weeks before he had escaped. These boys were rank amateurs and he knew he could take anything they threw at him and more.

'So, would you like to talk?' asked The Pastor.

Griff nodded and mumbled an incoherent sentence.

Again The Pastor gestured toward one of the henchmen who stepped forward, putting his face close to Griff's. 'Talk to me,' he said.

Griff repeated himself, mumbling for all he was worth.

The man leaned forward to try to make out what Griff was saying.

And the old veteran whipped his head forward. His forehead smashed into the henchman's nose with a satisfying crunch and Griff yelled out his satisfaction.

'Yeah,' he shouted. 'Take that, you asshole.'

The other man in the room didn't even wait for instructions before he started to beat on Griff, raining blows down on him like he was a piñata.

Just before he blacked out he wondered how long it would take Brenner to find him.

2

Brenner had been in Kentucky when he had gotten the call from Griff. The info on the satellite phone had been linked to the tracker Griff had swallowed and showed the veteran was somewhere in West Texas. Over one thousand miles and at least sixteen hours' drive away.

So Brenner had set off immediately, driving through the night without sleep. Desperate to find his friend before the tracker went off-line. And hopefully, also before the rising of the full moon when he would be forced to turn into an uncontrollable monster for the night.

The sun started to peek over the horizon and Brenner checked his watch. He had been on the road for fourteen hours straight and he was nearing his destination. Unfortunately, Griff's estimated time frame of twenty-four hours had been incorrect. In fact his signal had faded then cut out after only twelve hours.

But Brenner had sufficient info to know his friend was somewhere near the foothills of the Guadalupe Mountains. So he headed along the interstate, searching for any town near the last known signal.

Riding northwest he kept going in the general direction the last signal had registered, using dead reckoning as his navigational aid. The roads changed to single lane and finally to dirt tracks with no signage.

He slowed down, negotiating the potholes and ridges,

keeping an eye out for rocks. After a minute or so of riding he saw a car parked next to the road, nestled in a pull-off area. As he got closer he could see it was a sheriff's car. A white Ford Crown Victoria. On the door a single star and the word, Sheriff.

Brenner noted that there were no county markings or motto. Unusual but not unheard of.

As he rode past, the two deputies turned their heads to follow him but didn't otherwise move.

Half an hour of careful riding later, Brenner saw another car. This one a white Ford Explorer. Also, a single star, the word, Sheriff. No county identification, motto, or contact numbers. Again, the deputies watched him go by but didn't give chase or pull him over.

Twenty minutes later Brenner saw a sign. It was professionally done but not the usual Government Issue. "Pepperpot – 15 miles". Reflective white paint on a dark green background.

Minutes later he passed another sign that read, "Welcome to Pepperpot".

The town was bigger than he would have thought. The main road was still dirt, but the sidewalks were cobbled and the buildings looked like a Disney version of a Wild West town. Wood buildings, hand-painted signs, and old-fashioned window displays. Many of the shops had hitching rails for horses. But there were no gun toting cowboys. Instead a smattering of normal looking people went about their day-to-day business.

Brenner rode slowly through the town and was surprised to find the main road simply petered out into a rough dirt track at the edge of the town. So he turned and went back, looking for the local barber shop.

He reckoned the barber usually knew the local gossip. He could get a haircut and use it as an excuse to ask about anything strange that may have happened of late, without having to explain himself as he would if he approached the local law enforcement.

He glanced at his watch as he walked, reminding himself he had to leave with plenty of time before nightfall. He had spotted a few places on the way in where he could stay for the night and chain himself up.

Ready for his inexorable transformation into the monster he became at the beginning of every full moon.

The shop was easy to spot. Outside the classic red and white barbers pole.

Brenner pulled up, parked his bike next to the hitching rail and walked in.

A man in a white coat sat on one of the two barber chairs reading a newspaper. He was the only person in the room and when Brenner walked in he greeted him with a sigh and a surly look. As if he was offended by the stranger's custom.

'Looking for a trim,' said Brenner.

'Have you made an appointment?' asked the barber.

Brenner looked around the empty shop and raised an eyebrow. 'Seriously?' he asked.

The man in the white coat didn't say anything, he simply

stood and waited for Brenner to answer his question.

Brenner took a deep breath. 'No. Actually, I didn't make an appointment. I've just got into town and figured I'd take a chance you were free.'

The man shook his head. 'Sorry. No appointment, no haircut. There are rules, you know.'

'But there's no one here,' argued Brenner. 'Look. Empty.'

'Be that as it may, if your name isn't in the book then you ain't setting your butt down in the chair.'

'Okay,' returned Brenner. 'Could I please make an appointment?'

'Sorry, no,' said the man. 'We're fully booked.'

'You gotta be shitting me,' exclaimed Brenner.

'No need to be all aggressive, sir,' said the barber. 'Rules is rules. Now if you don't mind, right of admission is reserved and I'd like you to leave.'

'Fucking idiot,' mumbled Brenner as he exited, closing the door behind him and taking a right turn, figuring to walk along the street a bit and see if there was anyone else he could ask a few questions.

Before he had walked ten yards, both of the sheriff's vehicles he had seen earlier pulled into the main street. The Explorer stopped in the middle of the road and the Crown Victoria continued until it was level with him.

He kept walking, eyes ahead but the Crown Victoria edged in front of him and stopped. They had obviously followed Brenner in as he had last seen the car over an hour before.

The two deputies stepped out of the car and approached Brenner. They seemed alert but not especially aggressive. Merely two cops doing their job.

Brenner stood still and waited.

'Sir,' said the one deputy. 'Please put your hands on the roof of the vehicle and stand with your legs apart.' He gestured toward the Ford Victoria as he spoke.

'Why?' asked Brenner.

'We have received a complaint that you have been harassing one of the townsfolk. Acting in an aggressive and threatening manner.

Brenner smiled. 'Not true. I asked for a haircut and he refused. Told me I needed an appointment. So I left. Anyway, that was like a minute ago, what did he do, get straight on the phone, and report me for wanting a trim? Man, thank God, I didn't ask for a shave. What then, would I have been accused of murder?'

The deputy's hand moved to his holster. 'Sir, step forward and place your hands on the roof of the vehicle. Do it now.' Brenner sighed, stepped forward, and placed his hands on the car.

The deputy kicked his feet back a bit, making sure Brenner was off balance, forcing him to lean forward, his weight on his arms. He ran his hands over Brenner, frisking him for a weapon. Then he pulled his hands behind his back and ratcheted on a pair of handcuffs.

After that he opened the back door. 'Please get into the vehicle, sir.'

'Really?'

'Yes, sir.'

Brenner complied. He knew this was obviously a misunderstanding and there was no need to antagonize the cops.

Small town deputies were often overzealous in their interpretations of the law. It had happened to Brenner many times before and, he was sure, would happen again in the future.

He would apologize, they would tell him off, maybe issue a warning and he would be on his way. He had to get out of town in the next couple of hours at the latest.

The sheriff's car was clean. Unusually so. Brenner had been in the back of police cars before. Many times. They normally all had the same smell. Cheap cleaner overlaid by ingrained sweat, puke, and the acid tang of fear. This car smelled of cigarette smoke, burgers, and coffee.

Still, he couldn't complain. With his wolf-enhanced sense of smell he was pleasantly surprised not to have his nostrils assailed by the usual putrid odors.

The sheriff's office was at the beginning of the main street and the drive took a little less than thirty seconds. Brenner wondered why they didn't simply walk there.

The deputy stopped the car, exited, and opened the door for Brenner, instructing him to lead the way into the building. The office was like many others Brenner had seen in the last few decades. Clean and tidy. A charge desk. Corridors leading off to the right. An open-plan office behind the desk.

The deputy guided Brenner along the corridor. At the end was a steel-covered door. He opened it and pushed Brenner inside.

Interrogation room. A sturdy wooden table, bolted to the floor, a steel hasp fixed into the tabletop. A single steel seat on the one side. Also bolted down. Opposite, two slightly more comfortable chairs. Freestanding. The standard two-way mirror stretched along the one wall. A bank of overhead fluorescents buzzed slightly, giving off a blue-white light that bleached out all color and made everyone look like they were recovering from a bout of flu.

The deputy pushed Brenner into the seat then he opened the cuffs, pulled Brenner's arms to the front, reattached them, and clipped them to the hasp on the desk.

Then he left the room, pulling the door closed behind him.

Brenner waited, aware of the minutes ticking by. The approach of the night. He hoped they weren't planning on keeping him here for the duration.

Eventually, after an hour of waiting, the door opened and a man walked in. He was dressed in the same uniform as the deputies but he was older and Brenner picked up a sense of leadership about him. It was obviously the sheriff.

He pulled up one of the chairs and sat opposite Brenner. Neither of the men spoke for a while.

'Finally the sheriff nodded. 'My name is Sheriff Harris. You got a name?'

'Brenner. Ded Brenner.'

'What sorta name is, Ded?'

'Name my pappy gave me,' answered Brenner.

The sheriff pulled out a pack of cigarettes. Lit up. He didn't offer. 'So what you gotta say for yourself, Mister Brenner?' asked the sheriff. 'Storming into my town, threatening my people. Cussing and demanding.'

'No, sir,' answered Brenner. 'Simply passing through. Felt the need for a haircut but apparently you have to make an appointment, even if the place is emptier than a banker's heart.'

The sheriff took a long drag on his cigarette before he spoke again. 'You weren't just passing through,' he said. 'There ain't nowhere to pass through here to. This is the end of the road. And according to my deputies you headed here from the highway. Directly here, no detours. So you obviously came here with a purpose. Now I wanna know what that purpose is.'

Brenner thought before he answered. He didn't want to mention Griff in case it started to complicate things and the sheriff decided to keep him there past sundown. So instead he simply said.

'I got lost.'

The sheriff shook his head. 'No. You traveled along a dirt road for over an hour. You didn't take any turnoffs, didn't deviate. And when you got here you headed for the barber. Just the place I would have gone to if I wanted to get the lowdown on the local scuttlebutt. So, I say again, what you doing here, Mister Brenner.'

The sheriff lit another cigarette and waited for a response but Brenner didn't answer.

'Who are you working for?' asked the sheriff. 'FBI, Homeland Security? Private contractor?'

'Sorry, Sheriff Harris,' answered Brenner. 'I honestly have no idea what you're talking about. I'm just a drifter. I'm going from one place to another place. There's no ulterior motive, nothing deep or sinister. Just a man and his bike and the road.'

The sheriff puffed on his cigarette, his eyes fixed on Brenner. A patient man. No one spoke until the sheriff had finished his smoke. Five, maybe six minutes. An eternity of silence.

Then he stood. 'Fine,' he said. 'Maybe a night in the cells will reveal the truth.'

Brenner shook his head. 'No.'

The sheriff laughed. 'You don't get to dictate terms, boy,' he said. 'Either you tell me what I wanna know or you stay here until you do.'

The door opened and two deputies walked in. They had obviously been watching through the two-way mirror and had entered to take Brenner to a cell.

Brenner felt a wave of panic flow over him. He couldn't be here tonight. People would die. They didn't have a cell strong enough to stop the monster. For their sakes he had to get out.

Now.

Summoning his strength he took a deep breath and jerked his hands apart, shattering the handcuff's chain as he did so. Then he leapt up and headed for the door.

The sheriff jumped in front of him as he moved and Brenner shouldered him aside, trying not to hit him too hard as he did.

As he barreled into the sheriff he heard the sound of a gas cartridge being fired and he knew someone had fired a taser. Fifty thousand volts arced through him like a tsunami, shutting down his nerve endings, cramping his muscles, and sending his heart into overdrive. With a yell of defiance, Brenner turned and yanked the weapon out of the deputy's hand, bringing the assault to an end.

But at the same time the second deputy fired. Then the sheriff. One hundred thousand volts drove Brenner to his knees, at which stage the deputy whose taser he had removed, stepped over to him and hammered his baton into the back of his neck, smashing the big man to the ground.

The last thing Brenner registered was the taste of blood in his mouth and the overwhelming feeling of despair and guilt at what he knew was going to happen in a few short hours' time.

3

The alarm had sounded shortly after nightfall. About eight o'clock. It was connected directly to the sheriff's house. As it was to all the deputies as well.

Sheriff Harris arrived first. He took seven minutes to get from his house to the station and when he arrived it looked as though the building had been hit by an extremely localized tornado.

The double front doors had been blown off their hinges and lay in the street, buckled and broken. As he stepped inside he saw the charge desk had been smashed to kindling and a few of the office desks had been thrown around the room like a child's toys in a tantrum.

Two of the deputies arrived as Harris was hurrying along the corridor to the cells. He had left one of the deputies on duty. A young man by the name of Robin Dexter.

The door to the cell block had suffered the same fate as the other doors and it lay in pieces on the floor. The three policemen rushed inside to find Dexter lying on the floor, covered in blood. Harris knelt and checked the deputy's pulse. It was weak but he was still alive. Although it was obvious from the angle of his arms and legs that all his appendages had been broken. He was bleeding from a deep gash on his chest. It looked as though he had been hit by a Mack truck.

Harris turned to one of the deputies. 'Get the doc here.

Now.'

He rolled Dexter slowly over into the recovery position then stood and went to check on the cell in which Brenner had been incarcerated.

The cell door was built from double-ribbed interlocking one-inch-thick hardened steel bars. It was mounted on two industrial strength tracks and locked via an electronic lock with a manual override. Something had torn it off its mountings and cast it into the corridor.

Both Harris and the deputy stared at the bent, ruined steel door, masks of utter disbelief etched across their faces.

'How is that possible?' asked the deputy.

Harris shrugged. 'He must have had accomplices,' he said. 'Somehow, they got in, placed explosive charges and blew the door off.'

'And what about the other doors?' continued the deputy. 'And the desks. And Dexter? Also, there aren't any scorch marks. It looks as though something mechanical removed the doors. A battering ram, or something like that.'

Harris bent over to take a closer look at the gate. Then he pointed. Two of the bars had been bent totally out of shape and, if you looked closely enough, you could make out individual finger marks on them. As if someone had removed the door by simply grabbing it and tearing it off with pure physical effort. 'Are those handprints?' he asked, almost to himself.

'Impossible,' breathed the deputy.

'Yeah,' agreed Harris. 'But they sure do look like them.'

He stood. 'Right, I'm going to get hold of The Pastor. You get on the phone and get everyone here. The deputies, assistants, anyone who usually volunteers. Everyone. We need to find this asshole and we need to start looking ASAP because there's a reckoning to be had.'

4

Brenner surfaced slowly. He was lying on his back. It was daytime. He was not alone.

He opened his eyes and looked up. Above him, a faded tarpaulin, stretched between two poles and lashed to the side of an old Winnebago. He was lying on a thin camp mattress on the ground. Covered by a threadbare, but clean, woolen blanket.

Someone was smoking and he turned to look at the person. An old man of obvious Native American extraction. Long gray hair, clean shaven. Wearing a checked shirt, faded jeans, and a pair of hand-stitched moccasins.

He nodded at Brenner and spoke. *'Ya'at'eeh, Niish Wase'ekhaar'a.'*

Brenner shook his head. 'Sorry, dude,' he said. 'No idea what you just said.'

The old man laughed. 'I'm not surprised. Do you know at the last count there were less than a handful of people who still spoke the traditional language of the Wichita Indians? The youth of today care little for the customs of their ancestors.'

Brenner nodded. 'True,' he admitted. 'However, I still have no idea what you just said.'

'I said, greetings, Moon Wolf.'

Brenner sighed. 'So you know?'

The man smiled and held out his hand. 'My name is

Kohana Harjo. Some call me chief.'

Brenner shook his hand. 'Brenner,' he said. 'Ded Brenner, pleased to meet you, Mister Harjo.'

'Please, call me Kohana. Two of my braves found you a couple of miles from here. Butt naked. Two dead bighorn sheep next to you. Half eaten. Apparently, you have a penchant for their livers. They brought you back here this morning. So how long has the spirit of the wolf been a part of you?'

'I'm not a werewolf,' said Brenner. 'I'm the result of a genetic experiment carried out on me by the United States Army. They were trying to create a super-soldier, instead they got me.'

'Do you change on the first night of the full moon?' asked Kohana.

Brenner nodded.

'Can you change into a wolf or a Wolfman at will?'

Again, Brenner nodded.

'Are your strengths, your senses, and your healing powers enhanced even when you are in human form?'

'Yes.'

Kohana smiled. 'Well then, regardless of the wheres and whys and whats, the fact of the matter is, you are a werewolf. But if you would rather think of yourself as some sort of failed military experiment then that's your prerogative. But to us you are the *Niish Wase'ekhaar'a*, the Moon Wolf, and as such, our people, the Wichita, hold you in the highest esteem. We have a saying; to look into the eyes of the wolf is to see your own soul.'

'I thought you Wichita dudes lived in Oklahoma. What you all doing up here?'

'We live where we live,' replied the chief. 'We are not traditionally a nomadic people but we have assumed a nomadic lifestyle of late. Just this small group of wanderers. I suppose one might say we follow a different path. One which has been preordained for us.'

A young man entered the bivouac and nodded his greeting to Kohana.

'Greetings, esteemed one. I have come to see how the Moon Wolf is doing.'

Kohana gestured toward Brenner. 'As you can see, he is awake. Did you bring him some clothing?'

The man nodded and handed over a pile of neatly folded clothes to Brenner. 'Moon Wolf,' he said. 'My name is Machik. I am one of the men who found you this early morning. I am glad to see you are well. These clothes should fit, they used to belong to a man called Sormak before he passed, he was renowned amongst the Wichita for being a giant and these were his traditional clothes.'

Brenner stood and put the clothes on. A long, plain, pullover, cotton shirt in khaki. A pair of soft light-brown suede trousers with leather belt. There was also a pair of steel-capped workman's boots in scuffed black leather. Brenner picked them up and raised an eyebrow. 'Traditional?'

Machik smiled. 'Ahanu couldn't abide moccasins,' he

explained. 'Said he liked to have something substantial on his feet.'

Brenner pulled on a pair of socks and the boots. Amazingly they fit perfectly.

'Come,' said Kohana. 'The people are gathering for lunch. Join us.'

Brenner followed the two men. As he walked he checked out the surroundings. A group of seven Winnebagos formed a loose circle around a common area. Most of the motorhomes had a canvas lean-to attached as an extension to the property.

In the middle of the clearing stood a large trestle table surrounded by fold up seating for at least twenty people. Men, women, and children bustled around the table laying down plates, cutlery, bottles of iced tea, and pots of steaming food. The smell of the food made Brenner's mouth start to water and an involuntary growl escaped his lips.

And near the top of the table, seated next to each other, were two old men.

Both were dark skinned with long gray hair and blue eyes. Bushy gray beards, semi-formal clothing. Open-necked white shirts, dark suits, patent leather shoes. The clothes were neat and clean and so threadbare you could almost pick out the individual strands of the weave.

They were drinking a clear liquid and they raised their shot glasses to toast Brenner.

Brenner shook his head with disbelief. 'Mister Reeve,' he

greeted. 'Mister Bolin.'

'Wolfman,' they returned.

Brenner turned to Kohana. 'What the hell are these two old busybodies doing here?'

Kohana looked visibly shocked at Brenner's disrespectful tone. 'Please, Moon Wolf,' he replied. 'These are honored guests. For many generations the Watchers have been friends to the Wichita people. They are very important to us. I assume you have met before.'

Brenner nodded and sat opposite the two old men.

Mister Reeve slid a full shot glass across the table. Brenner tossed it back and held it out for a refill.

The rest of the table filled up, but people were silent as they waited to see what was about to transpire between the Moon Wolf and the Watchers.

'Brenner spoke first. 'So tell me something,' he said. 'Do you guys follow trouble or do you create it? I ask because for the last fifty years I've pretty much managed to stay ahead of the game. Kept my nose to the floor and stayed out of the crap. But since I met you guys it's been nonstop shit-creek time.'

Mister Reeve laughed. 'We don't create anything, son,' he said. 'We watch. That's all. We watch.'

'You watch? Well what the hell for? What good did watching do for anyone?'

Both Mister Reeve and Mister Bolin looked genuinely puzzled at Brenner's question. It was as if someone had asked what good breathing was.

'If I might explain,' interjected Kohana.

Mister Reeve nodded. 'Feel free, chief Harjo. To be honest I am at a loss as to why the Wolfman is ignorant of the concept, given his supernatural lineage, as it were.'

'What lineage?' asked Brenner. 'I'm a failed military experiment, as I keep telling you guys. Nothing supernatural about it, so there's no reason I'd be privy to any sort of extra information or understanding.'

'Fine,' said chief Kohan Harjo. 'It's actually real simple. You see, the act of observing validates the action. Does the moon actually exist if no one is looking at it? Who knows? Thereby the act of observation can create or destroy an entire planet. The watchers are extremely powerful beings. The modern world has forgotten how to watch. Through their impatience and need for instant gratification they belittle themselves. To watch, to observe, is to gain power. As opposed to the act of consumerism. People look at the world around them, but they do not observe. The act of watching is necessary for our continued existence. The act of watching validates us.'

Brenner shook his head. 'Deep,' he said. 'But not sure if it's my bag.' He turned to the two misters. 'So if you guys see everything, can you tell me where my friend Griff is?'

Mister Bolin shook his head. 'We never said we watch everything. That would be impossible. We watch the things that matter.'

'And how do you know what matters?' asked Brenner.

Mister Reeve chuckled. 'Well, as a rule, if we watch it,

then it matters. And in answer to your request, no, even if we knew, we cannot tell you where Mister Griffin is at the moment. Unfortunately we are the Watchers, not the Advisors. However, if you ask Chief Harjo for his help then I am sure he would comply. After all, the Wichita hold the Moon Wolf in very high regard. In fact they have even found your motorcycle and brought it here for you.'

Brenner turned to Kohana. 'Is that true?'

'About the Harley? Yes, two of my men found it in the town of Pepperpot, locked in the sheriff's compound. Under my instructions they brought it back here.'

'How did you know it was mine?' asked Brenner. 'And when it comes to that, how did you know where to look for it?'

Kohana smiled. 'We saw you riding into the area yesterday. As to how we knew where it was, well, everything of note that happens in this area seems to emanate from the town of Pepperpot. After all, it is the only place of collective dwelling for many hundreds of square miles.'

'Thank you,' said Brenner.

Kohana shrugged. 'It is of no moment. And as to the Watcher's suggestion that we help. Our time is yours, Moon Wolf. What would you have us do?'

'I seek a friend. He was kidnapped a few days ago and the last information I had showed he had been brought to this area. Close to here. But I am unsure of exactly where he is. I need to find him. And quickly. I have reason to believe his life is in imminent danger.'

The chief nodded. 'This is a very large area, and we are few,' he said. 'Is there any way of narrowing the search down somewhat?'

'I guess Griff would be in some secluded place. Off the grid. Whoever took him would have done so because Griff would have overturned some stone on the internet that revealed something dank and evil. So someone tracked him down and took him. As such, it would be a secret place. Or someplace strange. A cult, a secret facility. Could very well be government. Not necessarily hidden but definitely secluded and off-limits to casual visitors.'

'Let us all eat,' said Kohana. 'Then we shall discuss this puzzle amongst us all and develop a plan of attack.' He beckoned to all at the table. 'Eat, then we work.'

The people set to, eating, talking of inconsequential things, joking, laughing. A large family. Togetherness.

And Brenner felt a sense of belonging he seldom came across. It was a welcome change. A lift to his spirits and a balm to his troubled soul.

5

They had left Griff in the chair overnight. And if he had to be honest with himself, he was starting to take strain. Okay, these guys were rank amateurs when it came to torturing a dude for information. They showed no subtlety. No knowledge of the psychology of the whole thing. It was simply, punch, slap, ask questions.

But Griff knew he wasn't the same age he used to be back in 'Nam and although he could hold out for longer than they would have thought possible, he just hoped it would be long enough for Brenner to track him down. Because he knew that the moment they figured out he was no threat at all, they were definitely going to punch his ticket. End of the ride.

And although Griff knew his friend would move hell and high water to find him he had the added complication that last night had been the first night of the full moon. And unless Brenner had found a place to chain himself up securely then who knows what kind of shitstorm might have been unleashed by now?

If he had gone full monster in a town or any populated place then there was every possibility he had left a wake of dead bodies in his path. And if that was true, then by now there would be a massive police search going on. Hell, they might have even mobilized the home guard, thought Griff.

Then he smiled. If that was true then they had better have

ordered up a full brigade at least. Because Brenner wouldn't go down for a mere battalion strength attack. No sir. Not the Wolfman.

The door opened and The Pastor walked in with two of his henchmen. Griff noted with satisfaction the one assistant had two black eyes and a plaster cast over his broken nose.

He grinned and winked at the man. 'Nice look,' he croaked, his voice hoarse with dryness.

The Pastor carried a jug of water with him and he walked over and held it to Griff's lips. The old man drank greedily, sucking in water as fast as he could before it was taken away. But he needn't have worried as The Pastor kept the jug there until Griff had drank his fill.

'Right,' he said as he passed the empty jug to one of the henchmen. 'You've had a bit of time to think, Mister Griffin. Now are you going to tell us who you work for and what you know. And before you start I would like to say your trick with the virus in your hard drives, while clever, didn't work. Our computer techs are way beyond such obvious booby traps. Unfortunately, your wipe did take, so there was nothing for us to ascertain from the drives. As such, we need you to inform us of everything we need to know then we will let you go. Simple as that. You have my word.'

'Okay,' said Griff. 'As long as you promise I can leave afterward. I mean, obviously I won't tell anyone anything. I'll just go on my way and forget this ever happened. No harm, no foul.'

The Pastor nodded. 'Mister Griffin. You have my word.'

Griff took a deep breath. 'Right. I work for a secret government agency. My name is not actually Reece Griffin. Well, strictly speaking, it used to be, but I am now referred to only as Agent J. I was recruited by Agent K and together we protect the earth from intergalactic threats. We are known as ... the Men in Black.'

There was a slight pause then The Pastor lost his cool. He stepped forward and slammed his fist into Griff's face. Once, twice, three times.

Griff barely managed to stay conscious as blood poured from his already broken nose to add to the blood streaming from the new cuts above his eye and his lip.

'You think you are some sort of comedian?' screamed The Pastor. 'I'll knock the humor out of you, you stupid, arrogant piece of shit.' He hit Griff again, this time with an open hand, slapping his ear as hard as he could. 'You have mistaken my politeness for weakness,' he continued. 'And now you shall be punished.'

The two henchmen grabbed Griff. One detached his chains from the chair then they yanked him to his feet.

'Put him in the hotbox,' commanded The Pastor. 'We shall see how humorous he thinks that is after a couple of days.'

'Wait,' mumbled Griff through swollen lips.

The Pastor held up his hand and the two men stopped dragging Griff and held him still.

'What?'

Griff Smiled. Albeit a slightly twisted, shop soiled smile. 'You have no idea what is about to happen to you,' he said. 'I almost feel sorry for you.' He laughed softly. 'Almost.'

The Pastor struck him again and this time Griff passed out, the twisted smile still on his broken lips.

***

Griff awoke a few minutes later, his aching head thumping in time with his heartbeat. His hands were no longer chained. And although it was still early morning, the heat pounded at him like he was in an oven. He looked around to see he had been placed in a classic hotbox or sweatbox.

A six foot, corrugated iron cube with a stout door and a small viewing slit in each wall just below the ceiling.

Griff peeked out of the viewing slits. It seemed as though he was on some sort of farm. Fields stretched out all around. People stood in rows and swung hoes and pulled rakes. Old fashioned tools of wood and steel. They looked like prisoners. Chain gangs. But there were no actual chains.

They were all dressed identically in rough-woven gray smocks. As near as he could deduce he reckoned they were weeding between rows of soya plants. They looked fit and well-nourished even though their demeanors were of resignation and defeat.

There were mountains in the near distance. And to the

right he saw a row of rudimentary huts, almost shacks. He had been held prisoner in the shack at the end of the row. Two guard houses were situated equidistant from the center of the row of shacks, large windows, floodlights, and steel bars. Inside each one, two men with shotguns.

But there were no fancy buildings. Nothing someone like The Pastor would demand. So it was obvious there was more to things than just this set up. There must be someplace where the leader and his henchmen stayed. Perhaps another farm. Perhaps a separate area completely. Somewhere away from the peasants.

But who the hell are these people, wondered Griff. The whole set up reeked of being some sort of cult. But usually in any cult the leader stayed with the followers. One with his people. But instead of a leader these people had guards. Which meant, in all probability, they weren't a cult. They were being held against their will.

They also weren't part of a normal, legal labor force. No one signs up to do farm work with Iron Age tools while dressed as a medieval peasant.

And although Griff knew far less about these people than they suspected, he had been researching them on the net. Both the normal and the Dark Web. And that was purely because he had come across a number of hidden transactions while looking into the financials of a certain high-up politician. Large sums of money had been transferred from various different accounts to a numbered account in the Cayman Islands. Millions. And when Griff saw millions of unauthorized dollars changing hands his "Conspiracy Theory" button got pushed big time. But he had been overeager and it had led to a certain amount of clumsiness so they had become aware of his ingress, tracked him down and snagged him. An inexcusable rookie error on his part.

But there was one thing Griff was sure of, and that was—these guys weren't making the pile of bucks he had seen by farming soya. Not even if they were using slave labor. No ways.

With that fact in mind, the old man sat cross-legged on the floor and assumed the lotus position. Hands resting on his knees he emptied his mind as he strove for a meditative state. Because he knew, without some serious relaxation and meditation, he was going to struggle to stay alive in the oven the box was becoming.

6

The young bucks in chief Harjo's small group all owned trail bikes. Mainly different beat-up versions of 1990s Hondas, Kawasaki's, and Yamahas. There were eight of them in total and Kohana had sent them out to scout the surrounds, looking for any sign of where Griff might be.

'Look for anything unusual,' Brenner had instructed. 'Strange buildings, security fences, signs of guards. Anything.'

Brenner trusted the young men, with their local knowledge, would recon the area more efficiently than him.

After lunch, the bucks had taken off in a cloud of oil smoke and dust.

Coincidentally, the Watchers also disappeared after the midday meal. One second they were there, the next, not even the shot glasses remained.

Brenner, who had spent enough time in the military to know when to relax, went back to his bedroll and used the time to catch up on some sleep.

He woke an hour or so later to the smell of cigarette smoke. The chief was sitting near to him, pipe in hand. In front of him, on a small table, was a battered aluminum teapot. Brenner stood, walked over to the table, and sat in a chair.

Kohana nodded a greeting then pointed at the teapot. 'Want some?'

'What is it?'

'Green tea,' replied Kohana.

'Sure,' answered Brenner. 'Thanks.'

The chief poured and pushed the mug across. Brenner took a sip. It was a long time since he had last drunk any hot beverage besides coffee and he was pleasantly surprised. The tea was fragrant and complex with a sweet aftertaste. It was invigorating. Like he had just splashed cold water on his face.

'It's good,' he said.

Kohana nodded. 'Truth be told, it's not real green tea. Well, it is, but I have added some extra herbs.'

Brenner finished his mug and Kohana refilled it. 'So, Moon Wolf,' he said. 'Tell me, what do you do?'

Brenner shrugged. 'Nothing really.'

The chief chuckled. 'Not true,' he said. 'Unless you are a corpse in a sealed vacuum then you are always doing something. Even if it's just rotting away.'

'Oh, I thought you meant, for a living.'

'Okay,' conceded Kohana. 'Then what do you do for a living? How do you survive? Do you work, odd jobs, that sort of thing?'

Brenner shook his head. 'No. But I get by.'

Kohana raised an eyebrow.

'Nothing illegal,' stated Brenner. 'Well, that's not actually true. Maybe I should qualify the statement. Recently I got into an altercation with a bunch of corrupt people. I brought an end to their operation and during the process came across a substantial amount of cash. I kept some of it. A few months before a group of gangbangers tried to mug me. That didn't go too well for them. But it transpired they had just finished a remarkably good day. They had wads of cash on them. I relieved them of it. Before that, I got caught between two gangs of drug dealers duking it out. I put an end to the violence …'

'And relieved them of their ill-begotten gains,' interrupted Kohana. 'Yeah, I'm beginning to see a pattern here. I get it. So, apart from relieving criminals of their money, what else do you do?'

Brenner shrugged. 'I suppose I travel. I search. I run.'

'You run? What from?'

'Strictly speaking, I was never actually discharged from the army. So, to all intents and purposes, I'm still AWOL. And the guys who experimented on me are constantly looking for me. Hunting me down. They've gotten close a few times but no cigar.'

'And you mentioned searching,' continued Kohana. 'What do you seek?'

'A cure. A way to put an end to this affliction they have cursed me with. I don't suppose you could help? Any sort of ancient tribal knowledge? Some folk remedy?'

The chief looked visibly shocked and horrified. 'You have deemed your calling to be a curse?' he asked. 'Your ancestors have gifted you with the greatest of insight and power and you spit in their faces and call it a burden?'

'This has nothing to do with my ancestors,' argued

Brenner, amazed at the chief's reaction. 'This whole thing was courtesy of Project Bloodborn. All thanks to Uncle Sam. The United States Military.'

'So you say,' answered Kohana.

'Yes,' agreed Brenner. 'So I say. I got shot to shit in 'Nam. Took six to the chest. Should have died. Next thing, I wake up on a hospital bed in some sort of laboratory. Totally cured. Not even a scar. I tried to move but they had strapped me down. Thick leather straps, like I was a mental patient. Then the experiments started. No one spoke. Men in surgical masks. They took blood. They took skin samples. They cut into me and timed the recovery cycles. Deep cuts. Wounds that should have killed me. But they didn't. They all healed. They injected me with mind-altering drugs. Truth serums. Pain enhancers. Pain killers. Anything and everything they could think of.

And then one day, six dudes in full combat gear come to the laboratory. They wrap me in chains before cutting the straps. Then they toss me on a gurney and wheel me into this room. In the center of the room is a cage. Maybe twenty feet by twenty by ten. Steel bars as thick as your wrist. Real industrial strength stuff. They take off the chains and chuck me into the cage.

Some other dude sets up a couple of cameras and they leave, locking the door behind them. Big steel door.

I sit. I Wait.

Next thing I black out. Later I wake up on the floor of the cage, utterly exhausted.

A group of men surround the cage. They stare at me like I'm some sort of exhibit in a fucking freak show.

Then, without a word, they pull down a screen and show me the film footage of the night before.

It's me. And as I watch I see myself turn into a monster. A wild and savage beast. Attacking the bars, howling, barking, and roaring.

After hours I fall to the floor and change back. To me. Sergeant Ded Brenner. The soldier, the person. The fucking werewolf.

Then one of them finally spoke. And all he said was, *last night was the first night of the full moon. Welcome to Project Bloodborn, Sergeant Brenner.'*

Brenner patted his shirt for a cigarette but then realized he didn't have any with him. Noticing the gesture, Kohana took a pack from his pocket, shook one loose, handed it over. Brenner put it in his mouth and Kohana lit and let the man take a few puffs before he encouraged him to continue.

'Go on.'

'Long story, not worth telling. The short of it is Griff helped me escape, got me a flight home-side. I been running ever since.'

Neither man spoke for a while.

Then Kohana said. 'You seek a cure for something which is not a disease. It is like attempting to cure the need to breathe. Or think.'

Brenner shook his head. 'It's not just the turning every full moon,' he said. 'It's every day. I struggle constantly against the beast. The desire to fix every problem with violence. The need to be the Alpha in the room. The desperate urge to rend and to kill all opposition.'

'But you do struggle against it,' said Kohana. 'And you succeed. You are not an animal. You are an enhanced human being. You are more than what you once were.'

'And when one day I can no longer control it?' asked Brenner. 'One day when someone in a bar insults me and I take out the whole bar. The whole neighborhood. The whole town. Because I am capable of it. I have become a weapon of mass destruction. Even now, when I feel justified to fight, I hold some part of me back, in fear that something will break free and I can't stop.'

Kohana took a drag of his cigarette and leaned back in his chair. Then he spoke. 'There is a story about an old Cherokee Indian chief who was teaching his grandson about life. "A fight is going on inside me," he told the young boy, "a fight between two wolves. One is evil, full of anger, sorrow, regret, greed, self-pity, and false pride. The other is good, full of joy, peace, love, humility, kindness, and faith."

"This same fight is going on inside of you, grandson … and inside of every other person on the face of this earth."

The grandson pondered this for a moment then asked, "Grandfather, which wolf will win?"

The old man smiled and simply said, "The one you feed."

You see, sergeant Ded Brenner. The soldier, the person, and the werewolf, we all have boundless quantities of evil in us. But we manage to control it. As will you. You are stronger than most. Have faith. And strive to see your blessing for what it is. Rather than dwell on the negatives, feed the positives. Be the good wolf.'

Before Brenner could answer, one of the young bucks rode in and pulled up next to Kohana's Winnebago. He kicked his stand down and ran over.

'I think I may have found your friend,' he said to Brenner. 'Not far from here. A farm with armed guards.'

Brenner stood. 'Show me.'

7

Machik was the young buck who had come across the farm. Brenner had hitched a ride with him to within a mile of the place. Then he had told Machik to drop him off and return to the camp. The buck had refused, arguing that two men were better than one when it came to assailing a place. But Brenner had insisted, knowing the young brave wouldn't keep up with him. Also, as Brenner pointed out, this may not be where Griff was. Who knew what was actually going on until he had given the place a thorough recce.

Reluctantly, Machick agreed and Brenner waited until he had disappeared over the horizon before he stripped and placed his clothes in the rucksack he had brought with him. Next, he extended the straps as far as they could go and looped the rucksack around his neck.

Then he changed.

It was a thing of great beauty.

There was no crunching of bones and tearing of flesh, like we are led to believe by Hollywood films. No screams of agony and grotesque stretching of jaw and limb.

Instead it was an almost balletic metamorphosis from human to animal. A natural change from the man to the wolf.

And the end result was something more than both. A synergy that had created a magnificent being of power. A wolf the size of a horse.

Lupinotuum pectinem.

The werewolf.

Brenner put his nose down and ran toward the farm, keeping low and making use of the natural folds and humps in the landscape. Staying hidden. He knew it would be easier if he waited until nightfall but he had no idea if Griff was actually there.

And if he wasn't, then he had to get back to searching. If he was, then he had to get him out as soon as possible.

When he was still a hundred yards from the area he caught a familiar scent on the breeze. The hackles on the back of his neck stood up and an involuntary growl escaped from his throat. It was Griff. His friend was there and it took a huge amount of willpower to stop from simply running in and destroying everyone he saw.

Instead, he flopped to the ground and waited. Letting his adrenaline rush ease. Griff was there. He was alive.

But Brenner had no idea who was the enemy and who may be in a similar situation to his friend. At a rough guess he reckoned the workers must be there under duress. Even though they had not been shackled nor were there fences. However, there were armed guards. Not many, but enough to constitute a deterrent to escape. Unless, of course, the guards were there to protect the workers from outsiders.

Brenner crawled a little closer and decided to spend a little time watching. After ten minutes he was none the wiser. The workers seemed docile, well-fed and they worked hard.

The guards were another story. There were six of them. Two in each hut and another two patrolling the fields. Brenner assumed there must be another shift for the nights. They were slack. They chatted amongst themselves when they should have been watching the land around them. They smoked, they dozed. Useless.

But there were six of them and they were armed with shotguns. Not that Brenner considered six armed men to be any sort of deterrent at all. He was, however, worried about collateral damage. Six men shooting wildly could take out many an innocent farm worker.

Then he heard someone shouting. From the small metal hotbox in the center of the fields.

'Hey, any of you assholes gonna give me some water? Or is it part of the plan that I die of dehydration?'

It was Griff.

And Brennerwolf could wait no more. He sprang to his feet and sprinted for the hotbox, covering the ground at a rate of thirty yards a second. Approximately three times faster than a top Olympic sprinter.

As he got closer he let out a roar. Atavistic and primal, it shook the very earth with its volume. The workers threw themselves to the ground. As did most of the guards.

Brenner heard Griff shout at him from the hotbox. 'About time, Wolfman,' he yelled. 'I'm fucking dying here.'

Brenner didn't even bother to slow down as he hit the hotbox. He simply barreled right through it, making sure he didn't strike Griff on the way. The corrugated metal walls burst out away from the old man and left him standing in the open.

Two of the guards in one of the huts opened up on Brennerwolf, firing their pump-action shotguns as fast as they could. The wolf turned and charged toward them. Buckshot slammed into him as he ran but it had no effect. Then he slammed into the guardhouse, snapping and biting as he exploded through the walls. Tearing at the guards in a frenzied attack. Killing both of them instantly.

The rest of the guards sprang to their feet and ran, as did most of the workers.

'Catch one of the guards,' shouted Griff. 'We need to question him. I'm going to get some water.'

Brenner ran one of the guards down, clamped his arm with his massive jaws and dragged him back to the hut Griff had gone into. He smashed through the doorway to find Griff drinking from a jug.

Brennerwolf tossed the guard against the wall then sat back on his haunches and stared at Griff, his golden eyes like two searchlights.

Finally the old man stopped drinking. 'Thanks for coming, buddy,' he said. 'Now, if you don't mind, I need to have a chat with this guard dude. Have to find out where the head asshole has gone. He and I have got some serious payback to discuss.'

The wolf nodded his agreement.

Before Griff could even start to question the guard, the man threw his hands up and spoke, his voice quivering with fear. 'I'll tell you anything,' he said. 'Everything I know. Just please don't let that thing eat me. Please.'

'I'll do what I can to stop him,' answered Griff. 'But I can't guarantee anything. Just be as cooperative as you can be.'

The guard nodded.

'Right,' said Griff. 'Let's start with, where can I find The Pastor?'

8

The guard had told all he knew. And although it was not as much info as Brenner and Griff wanted it was enough to get on with.

Their first order of business was to sort out the prisoners on the farm. They had all run away after Brenner had attacked, but while Griff was interrogating the guard, most of them drifted back. Now small groups of them stood and sat on the perimeter of the property. It wasn't that they were curious or wanted to get involved, it was simply that they were in the middle of nowhere and had nowhere else to go.

So it was a case of taking their chances with a monster which seemed to be mainly interested in the guards, or spend the night out in the open with no food, water, or shelter.

Brenner had changed into the set of clothes he had in the rucksack around his neck and he walked outside, stood in the open and called the prisoners to him.

The guard had told them the prisoners were not actually being held against their will. In actual fact, he had said, they were supplicants and seekers after the truth. They were part of The Pastor's flock.

Griff had told him to stop talking shit and had smacked him upside his head for being such an asshole. Seekers after the truth don't need to be kept at gunpoint by armed guards, he had said, and the guard had no answer to such a simple and obvious truth.

As it so happened the guard had actually been telling a partial truth. The Pastor had started a church he called, "The Fellowship of Rightful Labor" and some of the people were faithful supplicants.

Truth be told it was most certainly a cult as opposed to a religion and its most basic tenet was, "hard physical labor and simple living brought great rewards in the next life". The rest of the rules were simple variations on, "do what The Pastor tells you or spend a few hours in the hotbox". And The Pastor's orders ranged from, work all day for nothing to, spend all night in my bed.

Needless to say, it hadn't been too long before some of the devotees started to rebel.

Hence the armed guards. And like many of these cults, while admission was easy, leaving was nigh on impossible.

Although the guard insisted there *was* a turnover of devotees, whether it was because they had left the movement, or simply traveled to another compound or, possibly, were just dead, he had no idea. He was just the piano player in the whorehouse and was not privy to what went on upstairs.

One of the ex-devotees approached Brenner, his attitude both nervous and apprehensive. As he got closer he removed his sun hat and kept his eyes down.

'No need to be afraid, buddy,' said Brenner. 'I will do you no harm. I simply came here to rescue my friend.'

The man stopped in front of Brenner but still did not raise his eyes. Brenner could see that the man was of Mexican extraction. He was much smaller than Brenner but he seemed to be both well-fed and healthy.

'*Buenas Tardes, senor.*'

Brenner nodded. '*Hola.*'

'*Senor,*' continued the man. 'I assume from the fact that only the old man, the guard, and the wolf went into the building then you came out that you must be *el hombre-lobo.*'

Brenner sighed and for once didn't bother with his usual, failed US Army experiment explanation. Instead he nodded and waited for the man's response.

'Are you, *Nahuale?*' the man asked, his face a mask of worry and concern.

Brenner was about to inform the man that he had no idea what he was talking about when Griff, who had just walked up beside him, answered in his stead.

'No,' informed Griff. 'He is *el hombre-lobo*. He means you no harm.'

'Well I'm glad that you know what's going on,' interjected Brenner. 'Personally, I have no clue as to what this dude is talking about.'

'He wants to know if you are a magician of some sort. Traditionally they consider the *Nahuale* to be evil. They're shapeshifters, primarily they turn into coyotes or wolves,' said Griff. 'You know, Ded, that's typical. You're the one who's been afflicted with the whole werewolf thing and I'm the one who has done the research and knows all about it.

Maybe sometime, instead of complaining you should spend a few hours on the net finding out more about it. Then perhaps you'd be less inclined to think so badly of the hand you've been dealt.'

'Whatever,' countered Brenner. 'Look, can you tell these dudes that we're outta here. Also, tell them The Pastor is soon to be referred to in the past tense only. I reckon this farm, in fact all the shit the so-called, "Fellowship of Rightful Labor" owns, is most likely off the books. So, tell this *hombre* they now own the farm. Appoint a leader, start their own fucking church, do whatever they want. Happy days and so on. Now let's go find the bad guys.'

Griff gave Brenner a stern look.

'What?' asked Brenner.

'Don't be a dick,' answered the old man. 'These guys have just been cut loose. They're scared and directionless. Not everyone can react like you, Ded. Most people need guidance. Why do you think they ended up joining this piece of shit movement in the first place?'

'*Senor*,' interrupted the Mexican. 'I did not join this movement. Neither did many of my *companeros*.'

'Well, how did you end up here then?' asked Griff.

The man looked embarrassed but answered nonetheless. 'There were a group of us trying to cross the border. We were caught by some border guards. As it turned out they weren't actual official guards. They were … how can we put it? Recruiting agents for The Pastor's cult.'

'Whoa, talk about frying pan and fire,' said Griff. 'How

long have you been here?'

'Not long, senor. Nobody stays very long. In fact some go on the first day. After the medical.'

'What medical?' asked Griff.

'Everybody undergoes a very extensive medical examination on their first day,' explained the Mexican. 'A large truck with many fancy machines inside comes and each person is vetted. If they fail the test, then they leave with the truck. We do not see them again.'

'What's your name?' Griff asked the Mexican.

'Antonio Martinez.'

'Okay, Antonio, you are now the official leader of this band of misfits. Brenner and I are going to leave you now, but we shall return in the near future. Or if not us then someone who we nominate. Is there anything you need?'

Antonio shook his head. 'No, *senor*. There is sufficient food and water here. Also, the guards keep a small amount of cash in the office. It is in a safe but that won't be a problem, I will get the surviving guard to open it before we lock him up. Also they have transport. All we ask is you ensure no one from that despicable church come here. However, even if they do, we have the guards' weapons now so they will not take us without bloodshed.'

'Good man,' said Brenner as he turned to Griff. 'All sorted?'

Griff nodded.

'Right, we have a general idea where The Pastor will be, let's take one of the guards' vehicles and get to hunting.'

Griff smiled. 'Yep, it's payback time.'

9

Brenner and Griff had taken one of the two vehicles from the farm. An old Ford Ranger that smoked like a Second World War battleship. But it seemed relatively solid, and as Griff said, it was better than walking.

They had followed the guard's directions and stopped around two miles from their end destination, traveling the rest of the way on foot so as to avoid detection.

Now they lay in the grass checking out the sprawl of buildings in the hollow below them. Like the last place they had just been at, this was also a farm. But that was where the similarities ended. Whereas the last farm was a perfect example of utilitarian construction, this was a study in luxury.

Workers tilled and weeded the fields. Mainly female workers, as Griff was quick to point out. In the background stood a copy of the classic Southern antebellum mansion, complete with a Byzantine dome and an army of Corinthian columns. The guards patrolled on horseback and the whole scene smacked more of the American South circa 1865 than the new millennium.

'Man,' noted Griff. 'This sick dude is living himself his very own personal fantasy.'

'Yeah,' agreed Brenner. 'Thinks himself to be the master of all he surveys.'

Griff shook his head. 'Come on. Let's go fuck up his day.'

Brenner didn't move. 'Are you sure you want to go through with this?' he asked.

'What do you mean?'

'I mean, once we start we can't go back. It's like I've said to you before, once I let the wolf out there's no turning back. Things get incredibly fucked-up, man. People will die, the wolf doesn't know how to be gentle.'

'Yeah, well, tough,' snapped Griff. 'Those assholes were going to off me, so you reap what you sow. Anyway, I want to find out what happens to those dudes who fail the medical exam. I also want to know why they even have such a thorough medical checkup. And why there's so much money being bandied about. This whole operation stinks, Ded. I think we need to crack it wide open and see what's inside.'

'Fine,' conceded Brenner. 'But let's wait until nighttime. I'd like the laborers to be in bed, less chance of collateral damage that way. Rest. Sleep a little. I'll wake you.'

Griff didn't argue and, like any ex-soldier, he took the opportunity to rest when he could.

Brenner continued to watch the farm until the sun slipped below the horizon. He didn't wake Griff, knowing the older man was exhausted after his two days of torture, dehydration, and lack of sleep. And there was no rush as Brenner wanted to wait until the laborers had eaten and were in bed, lights out.

Finally Griff woke up. He sat up, dry scrubbed his eyes with the back of his hands and nodded at Brenner.

'Anything of note happen?'

Brenner shook his head. 'Same old all day. Weeding, planting, picking. Guards prancing about on their horses. A plump dude with a shiny pink face came out onto the second-floor balcony for a while. Had a pair of binoculars. He spent a few minutes checking out the laborers then went back inside.'

Griff snorted. 'That's The Pastor. Pink-faced SOB. So, what's the plan?'

'No plan,' answered Brenner. 'The lights all went out about ten minutes ago. You wait here, I go Wolfman, neutralize the guards, grab The Pastor and call you.'

'No way,' argued Griff. 'I'm coming with.'

Brenner shrugged. 'If you want. How fast can you run the hundred?'

Griff laughed. 'Well, considering I've got a touch of rheumatoid arthritis, maybe thirty seconds. Maybe less. Why?'

'In Wolfman mode I can cross a hundred meters in less than three seconds. To put it bluntly, Griff my friend, when you get there the security detail will have had enough warning to erect a few barriers, call in the home guard and dig a series of ten-foot-wide trenches to stop us.'

'Hey,' exclaimed Griff. 'No need to be a dick about it. I'm getting old, you know.'

'I know,' said Brenner with a smile. 'And that is what it is, my friend. But the fact of the matter is, if I go in alone then I have a greater chance at sorting this out quickly and without loss of innocent lives. And by that, I mean, you or me. Or the laborers, I suppose.'

'Point taken,' admitted Griff. 'Fine then, go forth and conquer. Just make sure you don't inadvertently off, shiny pink face boy. I need to ask him some questions. By the way, how will you call me?'

'I'll howl,' said Brenner as he took his clothes off and packed them into his rucksack he'd hung around his neck. Then he took a deep breath and let the change take him. Skin and flesh rippled. Bone grew and hair sprouted.

Then standing there was a seven-foot-high Wolfman-hybrid. Shoulders as wide as a truck and teeth and claws larger than the saber-toothed tiger of old. A cross between man and wolf but so much more than a sum of its parts.

'Man,' said Griff. 'No matter how many times I see that it still humbles me. You, my friend, are one scary mother. Now go and do what you do best.'

Brenner growled and sprinted off into the night, disappearing in mere seconds as he ran toward the faux antebellum mansion.

Griff settled back and waited for the screaming to start.

10

It was a large room. Against the far wall, a bed. Massive. At least ten feet by ten feet. As big as some New York apartments. Above the oversized bed, suspended from the ceiling at just the right angle was a mirror of matching size. Subtly concealed mood lighting painted the walls in shades of fallen-angel scarlet.

A young woman stood in the middle of the room. She was naked, but she attempted to cover herself with her hands. She looked at the floor, eyes almost closed, mouth a tight line, her slightly elevated breathing the only obvious sign of her fear.

Standing in front of her was The Pastor. His round face slick with sweat. In his right hand a riding crop. Like the woman, he too was breathing heavily. The difference being that his heightened respiration was not a sign of fear. It was anticipation.

'You have sinned,' he said, his voice only slightly above a whisper.

The woman shook her head.

'Do not deny it,' said The Pastor. 'Denial only makes it worse. Open your heart and mind to the Lord and your punishment will be swift and just. As will your reward.'

The woman shivered in disgust and fear but said nothing. She had been here before and knew there was no point. He would beat her—punishment. Then he would rape her—

reward.

The Pastor removed his jacket and laid it on a chair next to the woman's discarded homespun smock. Then he approached her and raised the crop.

'Stand up straight,' he commanded. 'Arms by your sides. Let me see your disgrace. Do not try to hide the sites of your sin.'

The woman complied, and The Pastor licked his lips as he stared at her nakedness.

He raised the crop a little higher.

It was then they heard the first scream. It was a voicing of true terror like nothing either of them had ever heard before. It was the very vocalization of horror.

A roar shattered the night. Primal and pure. A sound that grabbed humanity by its amygdala and rang the bells. Fear, survival, paranoia. It reduced man to his primal essence, tearing away all remnants of modernity and leaving only those base instincts necessary for his continued existence.

The woman fell to the floor as her limbs refused to function and The Pastor let out an involuntary screech of fear, dropping his crop to cover his ears like a small child trying to block out the wail of the bogeyman.

The door to the bedroom burst open and two guards ran in. Both were wielding pump-action shotguns. One turned and covered the open door while the other ran up to the pink-faced man.

'Pastor,' he yelled. 'Something has broken in to the house. I called for help but it appears as if the rest of the guards have already been neutralized.'

Before The Pastor could react, the guard at the door flew into the room and struck the wall above the bed with such force, the sound of his breaking bones was clearly audible.

The other guard opened up, racking his shotgun, and firing as quickly as he could. After five rounds he was out. He dropped the weapon and pulled out a knife. An eight-inch Bowie.

'Come on,' he shouted. 'Come and get some.'

The Wolfman walked through the door, crouching slightly, and turning sideways as he did so to fit. He stared at the guard, his yellow eyes seeming to flay the very skin from his flesh with their power.

The guard dropped the knife and fell to his knees. 'Please,' he said. 'Don't …'

Brenner lashed out, striking the kneeling man in the jaw, breaking it, and knocking him unconscious. Then he turned to face the woman who was lying on the floor in the fetal position, her hands covering her eyes, her whole body shivering with dread.

'Do not be afraid,' growled Brennerwolf. 'I have come to release you, not to harm. Do you have clothes?'

The woman glanced up and nodded.

'Get dressed,' continued Brenner. 'Then leave. Do not worry about the guards. They are no more. Tell everyone else to fear not. Their subjugation is near to an end.'

The woman stood on shaky legs, walked over to a chair, picked up her rough smock, pulled it over her head, and left the room. As she walked through the door she turned to face Brenner, bowed slightly then whispered her thanks.

Brenner said nothing.

When she had left he leaned over and grabbed The Pastor by his shirtfront, lifted him up to his face and stared deep into his eyes.

Then he threw back his head and howled.

The Pastor literally soiled himself.

11

The Pastor was naked. And tied to a chair. With a well-used sock in his mouth.

'Why naked?' asked Brenner, who had changed back into a human and had dressed in the clothes the Wichita had given him.

'Because he's a shit,' answered Griff. 'He had that girl butt naked and now he is. *Quid pro quo.*'

'And the sock?' continued Brenner.

Griff shrugged. 'I know it's a bit childish, but I thought it was funny.'

'Marginally,' admitted Brenner. 'So, wanna take the sock out and start questioning him?'

Griff ripped the sock out and punched The Pastor hard in the nose. 'There, now your nose is fucked as well as mine.'

The Pastor said nothing. Instead he simply stared at Brenner, his eyes two round circles of fear.

Brenner took a step toward him and The Pastor started to literally gibber in terror. Incoherent squeaks and voicings. Like an old vinyl record being played backward at double speed.

Griff shook his head. 'I break the dude's nose and he's so petrified of you he doesn't even notice. Man, does this happen often?'

Brenner nodded. 'Always. Usually it's not so extreme a reaction, but, yes, they all crap themselves to a greater or lesser extent. The Wolf leaves a mark. It enters parts of their minds that typically hide in the dark and it rips them into the open. It exposes their innermost fears.'

'Well this dude is useless to me like this,' noted Griff. 'He's almost catatonic with terror. What do you normally do at this stage?'

'Not much you can do. Sometimes I just change back into the Wolfman then I eat them. Alive,' answered Brenner with a surreptitious wink at Griff.

The old man rolled his eyes while at the same time The Pastor let out a high-pitched squeal. Like a toy steam engine.

Griff walked over and slapped him. Hard. 'Now listen up, asshole,' he began. 'Pull yourself together. I am going to ask you some questions and you are going to answer. If you don't then things are going to get really bad for you. To be honest, actually, I don't see an ending where things could possibly work out good for you, but at least you have a chance. Answer fully and honestly and I'll see what I can do. You got it?'

The Pastor seemed to calm down a little and nodded.

'Okay,' said Griff. 'Firstly, why the medicals on the newcomers?'

'We like to ensure everyone is healthy,' answered The Pastor. 'The body is the temple of the Lord.'

'And the ones who fail the test? The not-so-healthy ones. Where do they go?'

The Pastor's eyes flickered up to the left and he hesitated

slightly before he answered. 'They are given a choice to get free medical help or to go back to their old lives.'

'He's lying,' said Brenner. 'You want I should eat his face off?'

The Pastor cringed and started to pray. 'Our Father, who art in heaven …'

Griff stepped forward and backhanded him. 'No,' he shouted. 'You do not get to pray. I have no idea what you are doing with this set up, but I know you're up to something bad. And as such, you don't get to call on Him. Now answer the question or I unleash the Wolfman.'

The Pastor quivered in his seat but didn't answer.

Brenner leaned forward, held his right hand up in front of The Pastor's face and, slowly, let his claws extend. They made a sound like a sword cutting through silk as they grew out, six inches of razor sharp keratin as hard as steel.

The Pastor took one look and started to talk.

'We release them,' he spluttered in his haste to get the words out. 'They are no use to us so we release them.'

'What do you mean?' asked Griff. 'Like, into the wild sorta thing.'

The Pastor shook his head. 'No. Spiritually, we release them. We free them from the bonds of earth.'

Both Griff and Brenner stood for a while, attempting to work out what The Pastor was talking about.

Eventually Griff did a double take. 'Do you mean, you kill them? You put them down?'

The Pastor nodded.

Griff wound up and punched the man so hard the chair fell over backward. 'You son of a bitch,' he yelled. 'Someone fails a medical and you kill them. You fucking Nazi. I ought to kill you right now, but I need more info.'

He yanked the chair up and put his face close to The Pastor's before he asked his next question. 'Right, fuck head,' he said. 'No more assing around, tell us what the hell is going on around here. I want to know everything. Talk. Why the medicals, why all these people, and why is there so much money floating around out there that I can connect to this so-called church of yours.'

'When I started, "The Fellowship of Rightful Labor" it was a genuine church,' said The Pastor. 'I was a lay minister in the southern Baptists and I found myself at odds with the teachings. They were too soft on the weak. Too liberal. So I collected a small group of likeminded faithfuls and we moved to this here farm I had inherited from my parents some two years before.

'Together we started our own church with me as the head Pastor. I advocated hard labor and frugal living as the best way to commune with the Lord and my followers agreed.'

'I assume this hard labor and frugal living didn't apply to you, fat boy,' noted Griff.

'I had a different calling,' admitted The Pastor. 'My calling was for leadership, not physical hardships. Anyway, it didn't take long and we found ourselves to be in financially dire straits. I hadn't paid the taxes on the farm, we were getting low on food and were far from self-sufficient. So we prayed and asked the Lord to provide for us.

'It was then that the father of one of our supplicants came to visit. At first, I saw him as an ungodly man. To put it bluntly, a criminal. His daughter had run away from him, citing his penchant for violence and his desire for control as her reasons. But, as we spoke, I saw the Lord does indeed work in mysterious ways.

'This man, this so-called criminal, showed me a way to not only protect but to increase my congregation. A way that would save lives as well as introduce more needy souls to God's grace.'

'Get to the point, Pastor,' snapped Griff. 'I'm getting a little tired of the whole godliness thing, so get to the meat of the matter or it's face-chewing time.'

The Pastor nodded. 'Fine, to put it shortly, this man knew people who needed help. Sick people. I mean, physically sick. Dying. And he saw a way we could help them to live. In return he would gift our church vast sums of money. Enough to expand over the years to become a real force for good in the world.'

'Hold on,' interjected Brenner. 'I'm losing the plot here. Are you saying you would ask God to cure these people then they would give you money?'

'In a way, yes.'

'What do you mean, in a way? Yes or no.'

'Although the Lord was definitely involved, these people, these very sick people, were not cured through the power of prayer. What these people needed were transplants.'

'Transplants?' questioned Griff.

'Yes. Kidneys, liver, bone marrow, that sort of thing.'

'And the donors?' asked Griff. 'They do it willingly?'

'They do so with the blessing of the Lord,' answered The Pastor.

'That doesn't answer the question,' snapped Brenner. 'Are the donors voluntary or are they coerced?'

The Pastor didn't answer.

'Oh, fuck it,' shouted Griff. 'I'll just go and get a few of them and ask. And if I find you were lying about anything, or if you were hiding anything, your death will take place over days, Pastor. Days of absolute agony. So decide now, are you going to tell the whole truth or not?'

The round-faced man seemed to deflate even further than he had already. His eyes welled up with tears and he lost the ability to keep his body upright, sagging against his bonds as he slipped down in the chair.

'We didn't only supply kidneys and livers,' he whispered. 'They needed more. Much more. Hearts, lungs, ligaments, bones, skin.'

'But a person can't donate that sort of shit and live,' said Griff.

'Obviously,' verified The Pastor.

Griff went pale, grabbed a chair, and sat. He was speechless.

'You were killing people and harvesting their body parts,' said Brenner. 'You fucking sick bastard.'

'No,' denied The Pastor. 'I helped to save lives.

Sometimes the parts from one person could save up to three, maybe even four other people. The many benefited from the death of the few. I was a savior, not a killer.'

'Oh, man,' said Griff, his voice hoarse with emotion. 'You are so fucked, dude. People are gonna celebrate your death for years to come.'

'Wait,' shouted The Pastor in desperation. 'You don't understand. The World Health Organization estimates only ten percent of global needs for organ transplantations are being met. Over one hundred thousand people in the United States alone die from the lack of donors. I am cutting that down.'

'And murdering innocent people while doing it,' yelled Griff. 'Not to mention lining your own pocket to a huge degree. I didn't manage to track all the payments down but you must be making millions. What the hell do you charge for this shit?'

The Pastor shrugged. 'It varies. Around fifty thousand for a kidney. Same for a liver. Double for a heart. More for a set of healthy lungs. Then there's eyes, spleen, marrow, blood, skin.'

'Enough,' said Brenner. 'So you make about one million a murder?'

The Pastor shook his head. 'Not even close with the amounts people demand for bribes. Doctors, lawyers, politicians. Then there's the sales commission. It's scandalous.'

Griff stepped forward and hit The Pastor again, once

more knocking his chair backward onto the floor with the strength of his punch.

'Careful, buddy,' said Brenner. 'You don't want to kill him. Not yet at any rate. Still got questions.'

'True,' admitted Griff as he pulled The Pastor upright.

'Right then,' said Brenner. 'Tell me, are there any other farms apart from this one and the one we have already seen?'

The Pastor shook his head. 'We only have two locations.'

'Fine,' continued Brenner. 'So how does the whole process work? I don't see any hospital here. Where do you harvest the organs? Where do they go from there? 'Fess up, asshat.'

'After they have worked in the fields for a while, living on a low fat, healthy diet to maximize the worth of their organs, the chosen are then taken by airplane to Mexico. We have an airstrip a short way from here. They end up at a private medical facility outside a tiny village called Los Juguetes. I don't know what happens from there on in. I get paid per person. There is no need to know what happens after I have delivered them. The Lord does not require that of me.'

'Los Juguetes?' confirmed Brenner.

'Yes. It is all I know. I swear, I have told you everything. Please, don't eat me.'

Brenner walked over to the fallen guard who had still not moved, and he picked up his discarded shotgun. Then he bent over and frisked him, removing a handful of cartridges from his pockets and loading them into the weapon.

'I reckon you hit that guard harder than you thought,' said Griff. 'I don't think he's actually still breathing.'

Brenner checked the man's pulse. 'Oops. Oh well, live by the sword and so forth.'

'What are you going to do now?' asked The Pastor.

Brenner didn't answer. Instead he simply raised the shotgun and pulled the trigger. The double aught shot smashed into The Pastors right knee, almost severing the leg as it blew his patella apart.

The trader of body parts screamed in agony.

Brenner waited until the man had stopped wailing then pulled the trigger again. This time The Pastor's left elbow disintegrated.

He screamed again, throwing himself from side to side as he tried desperately to escape his bonds.

'Mercy,' he screeched. 'I beg you, have mercy.'

'I am not a merciful man,' said Brenner. 'Especially not to filth like you who murder people for money.'

The Pastor looked beseechingly at the big man, his eyes running with tears. 'Please.'

Brenner shook his head and pulled the trigger again. And again. Then he turned to Griff. 'Come on, let's go. He won't last long.'

Brenner walked out of the room.

Griff stopped next to The Pastor, taking in his shattered limbs. Brenner had taken out both of the man's knees and elbows. It was only a matter of time before he died of shock or loss of blood. Either way, he was a dead man.

Griff shook his head. 'Well,' he said. 'You can't say I didn't warn you.'

12

Griff took another swig from his bottle of beer, followed by a drag of his cigarette. Then he leaned back in his chair and closed his eyes in near bliss.

They had arrived at chief Kohana's camp just after midnight and had spent the last two hours telling their story to the group.

This had mainly consisted of Brenner giving a quick rundown of the facts and Griff telling a yarn suitable for turning into a Game of Thrones epic. One where Brenner featured prominently, silhouetted against the moon, moving through the night like a vengeful shadow, and delivering both justice and retribution with an even and fair hand.

Needless to say, Griff's version of the night's events was more popular than Brenner's bald statement of reality.

'So what now?' asked Kohana.

'There are a couple of salient facts we both left out,' admitted Brenner as he grabbed his rucksack, opened it, took out a brown paper bag and placed it on the table. He proceeded to tear it open and allow the contents to spill out.

A couple of the younger men gasped.

Twelve bricks of plastic-wrapped dollar bills. Hundreds. A total of one hundred twenty thousand dollars.

'We found a safe in The Pastor's office. When Griff opened it we counted just over one million dollars. I took this and we left the rest for the people there. I also went and picked up Antonio and a couple of people from the first farm and introduced them all. I rigorously advocated that they run the two farms as a collective using the money to fund the whole thing. I also told them to use it to repatriate anyone who wished to go back home.

'You think they will listen?' asked Kohana. 'One million dollars can create a lot of enmity. People kill for a lot less.'

'I am confident they will do the right thing,' interjected Griff. 'After all, they saw Brenner in his full glory, and that tends to put the fear into anyone with even half a brain.'

'Plus,' added Brenner as he pushed the pile of money across the table to the chief. 'We were hoping you would keep an eye on them for a while. Give them a helping hand, pass on a few pearls of wisdom, that sort of thing. We would greatly appreciate it.'

Kohana smiled. 'Of course,' he agreed. 'And the money is not necessary.'

Brenner shrugged. 'It is or it isn't. Take it. Use it. Spread it amongst yourselves. Whatever, it isn't charity, it is payment for a job I know you will do well.'

Kohana nodded and pulled the pile of cash toward him. Acceptance of the payment. 'And what do you and Griff plan to do now?' he asked.

'Mexico,' answered Brenner. 'A place called, Los Juguetes. The Pastor says that's where they send the people that are gonna be sliced and diced for their organs. Griff and I reckon that maybe we go there and fuck the place up a little. See where that leads. But first we have another problem. A potential big one.'

'What?' asked Kohana.

'The sheriff,' answered Griff. 'Not only did Brenner bust up his jail and put the hurt on one of his boys, Antonio informs us the sheriff and his department are intricately involved with The Pastor. Or were when the shithead was still alive. They hunted down escapees, helped with security, kept outsiders from interfering. He's definitely going to visit and cause a large amount of shit to go down.'

'So what do you suggest we do about it?' asked Kohana.

'To be honest,' said Griff. 'I'm not sure. Brenner advocated his usual, find them, destroy them, method of conflict resolution. However, you off a bunch of cops, no matter how guilty they are, you gonna bring down heat. And we don't need that. The farms don't need it either. Somehow we have to discourage the sheriff from getting involved without ripping his head off.'

No one spoke for a while as they attempted to formulate some sort of plan to stop the sheriff intervening.

Finally Kohana said. 'Theater.'

'What?' questioned Brenner.

'We need to put the fear of god, or more accurately, the fear of the darkness into our sheriff. And I think I have an idea on how to do it.'

He told them his plan.

13

The sun had set and they waited at the side of the road. Hidden in the local scrub and brush. It was a narrow, ragged dirt track leading directly to the sheriff's house. A sprawling bungalow that stood alone on around two hundred acres of land.

And the sheriff was driving home at his usual time. Just before seven in the evening and some twenty minutes after sundown.

The chief and six of his men were dressed in traditional tribal wear. Tanned-hide shirts, loincloths, and leggings. Moccasins on their feet. Bow and arrows strung across their backs. Simple feather head dresses. Their faces had been painted with intricate lines and dots done in charcoal and mud and the area around their eyes had been darkened with the same charcoal. In the dark they looked more like apparitions than men.

Eyeless dead relics from days gone past.

Shadow warriors.

Off to the one side and further back lay Griff with a rifle. He was their, "just in case" backup.

Brenner stood with the Wichita. He was naked, not even carrying his usual rucksack with change of clothes. He had left it with Griff.

As the sheriff's vehicle came around the corner Brenner changed into his Wolfman form and ran straight at the side of the car as it passed. He connected with his shoulder and drove hard, smashing into it, and flipping it onto its side as he did so.

Then he moved back, standing in line with the rest of the Wichita men.

At the same time, Griff pulled the tabs on two smoke markers. One red and one white. The light wind shepherded the smoke toward the line of men and Wolfman, shrouding them in a blend of red and white.

Ethereal.

Unearthly.

The gibbous moon added just enough light to see forms and shapes but not features.

The passenger-side car door opened and a groggy sheriff clambered out and stood next to the vehicle. It took him a few seconds to register that all was not as it should be, and he stared open mouthed at the apparitions standing in the smoke.

Then Brenner roared. Long and loud.

The sheriff dropped to his knees and covered his ears with his hands but Brenner didn't stop. He roared again then threw his head back and howled.

When the sheriff finally looked up at him, he changed from Wolfman to full wolf and walked slowly toward him. Moving in a line with the Wichita warriors until they had surrounded him.

The smoke wafted and billowed, and the moon bathed all in a graveyard blue. And the eyeless men looked down at him, their bows and arrows at the ready, while the golden eyes of the huge wolf stared into his very soul.

Then the old Indian spoke. And while he did the other eyeless men chanted in counterpoint, their voices low and guttural. And the wolf growled along with them.

It took all he had for the sheriff to maintain his sanity and his sphincter control, such was the supernatural terror he was feeling. An overwhelming tsunami of absolute horror and disbelief.

'The Pastor is no more,' said the Indian. His voice expressionless. Devoid of feeling and emotion. 'The farms are under the shelter of the ancestors of the Wichita. They are protected by the great wolf. No longer will they be molested or harmed in any way. If you contact them again you will suffer a fate that will make death seem like a good thing. Do you understand?'

The wolf howled again, this time so loud the sheriff thought his eardrums would burst. The sound too loud to be natural. Too harsh to be anything else than paranormal.

The sheriff nodded. 'I understand.'

Then the wolf lunged at him, its massive jaws snapping together like a bear trap, mere inches in front of his face. The sheriff fell back and rolled, whimpering in terror as he did. His eyes tight shut. His sphincter control deserted him.

When he opened his eyes they were gone.

He sat on the ground, still, unmoving, for at least ten minutes before his legs could support him. Then he staggered over to the smashed car and called the station.

He made no mention of the wolf. Or the Indians.

Not then.

Not ever. How could he? People would think him a madman.

Nor did he visit the farms again. He never even contemplated it.

14

'You do realize neither of us have a valid passcard or passport,' said Griff.

Brenner nodded.

'So,' continued the old man. 'How were you planning to get into Mexico?'

Brenner shrugged. 'Honestly? I was hoping you would figure out a way. I mean, I haven't been there for forty years or so. To the best of my knowledge isn't there a fence, or wall, or some shit like that so you can't just stroll across. Border guards as well.'

Griff laughed. 'No, not really. There's about seven hundred miles of walls and fencing along the border. But there's still well over one thousand miles of no fence. But it doesn't mean you can just stroll across. Apart from the border guards, there's what they call a virtual wall. Cameras, motion detectors that sort of thing. It's a joke, man. If I can get a laptop with a satellite dongle I can hack in to their system, take down the virtual wall. Then as long as we don't get shot, we can get across.'

'I can give you a laptop,' informed Kohana. 'Also, I have something else for you, Griff.' He laid two leather cases on the table and slid them across to the old man.

Griff opened the smaller one. Inside was a Taurus .357 magnum revolver in matte stainless steel and a four-inch barrel. Also, two speed loaders and eighteen rounds of ammunition.

'A man needs a gun he can conceal,' explained Kohana.

Griff smiled. 'Thanks, dude. Very thoughtful of you,' he said as he opened the longer case.

It contained an old Mossberg 30-06 rifle with a matching scope and a box of twenty-five rounds.

'And that is because a man also needs a gun when you don't necessarily need to get up close and personal with the target.'

Griff shook the chief's hand. 'Thank you, man,' he said. 'I do truly appreciate this. And I am sure they will both come in useful.'

'We'll take the Range Rover we liberated from The Pastor,' said Brenner. 'You plan our route, we can bang it into the satnav and be on our way. I'll come back sometime in the near future to pick up my bike.'

While Brenner was speaking one of the young men brought Griff an Apple laptop complete with a dongle. The old man linked up and spent the next ten minutes checking out the virtual wall and surrounds.

'Right,' said Griff. 'I've got a kick-off point. You drive and I'll keep working on it, but I have the general area so let's get going.'

Goodbyes were said and the two men went on their way.

Griff put some coordinates into the satnav and headed south, sticking to the major roads for the first part of the trip. After a while Griff directed Brenner onto lesser traveled side roads and, not long after, onto mere dirt tracks.

Around ten miles from the border Griff got Brenner to leave the tracks completely and strike out across the open land, heading in a southwesterly direction.

After an hour of crawling along, he told Brenner to stop.

'Right,' he said. 'We wait here until it gets dark, then I'll direct you. Take a nap.'

Brenner nodded and took the opportunity to catch up on some rest.

Ten minutes after sundown, Brenner woke up and they continued on their way.

'I've disabled the cameras and the motion detectors,' said Griff. 'I'm not sure how long before they notice, or how long until they send someone. Can you drive with the lights off?'

Brenner nodded. 'Even without changing, I can see pretty well in the dark.'

'Good,' said Griff. 'That should get us through without picking up any unwanted attention. Head that way,' he pointed.

Brenner engaged the four-wheel drive and followed Griff's instructions.

It took a little longer than Brenner expected but, after a couple of hours of crawling through the dark, Griff announced they were a mile inside of Mexico. It was both anticlimactic and a relief at the same time.

'Where to now?' asked Brenner.

Griff pointed. 'This Los Juguetes is truly in the middle of

nowhere,' he said. 'If we head east we should cut across the only road in and out of the place. I mean this town is seriously between fuck and all.'

'Probably why they put their slice and dice shop there,' observed Brenner. 'No prying eyes, but has electricity and enough access to transport. Although I'd guess the organs are flown out, not taken by road.'

'Could be,' agreed Griff. 'Personally, I have no idea how long an organ lasts after you take it out.'

'Me either,' admitted Brenner.

The SUV bounced along the road for another hour. They avoided the ruts and potholes whenever possible, but it was still a bone jarring experience and when they saw a sprawling group of buildings in the distance Griff asked Brenner to pull over when they got there to see if there was a bar or restaurant.

As it happened there was a building that seemed to approximate a bar of sorts. A row of ancient, battered pick-up trucks were parked in front of it meaning it had some sort of clientele.

There was a hand-painted sign outside, but it was so faded and scarred by the weather that the only letters visible were an S and a T. It gave no clue as to what the original sign said and neither Griff nor Brenner were avid Scrabble players so they didn't bother to attempt to work it out, instead they simply pulled up outside, got out of the Range Rover, and walked into the building via the swing doors at the front.

The bar was of a type. Counter along the far wall. Behind that, shelves full of bottles of various alcoholic drinks. In this case mainly tequila.

A barman, rough shaven, a once-white shirt that was now a subtle shade of yellow-gray. Sweat stains under the arms with a demarcating line of salt at the perimeter of each damp patch.

In his hand a filthy cloth he insisted on using to vigorously polish each glass before he used it.

Seven or eight patrons sat at tables on mismatched chairs. Probably farm laborers. Perhaps factory workers.

'Where do these dudes work?' whispered Griff. 'I mean, we're slap bang in the middle of nowhere. Hell, this place is ten miles further up from the asshole of the world.'

'Maybe they're out of work,' answered Brenner. 'Who knows?' He walked up to the bartender. 'Hi. You serve food?'

The man nodded without actually looking at Brenner.

'Good. What you got?'

'*Sopa di frijol.*'

'Great,' said Griff with a sigh. 'Bean soup. Anything else?'

The man shook his head. '*Sopa de frijol,*' he repeated in a bored voice.

'Fine,' said Brenner. 'Give us two. Large helpings with a load of bread. Also a couple of beers. Domestic.'

'We only got domestic. In fact we only got Carte Blanca.'

'That'll do,' said Brenner.

The barman grabbed two bottles from the refrigerator,

opened them, and slammed them on the bar. Then he shouted out loudly. 'Maria. *Sopa de frijol. Y pan. Muchos.*'

The food appeared remarkably quickly, obviously ladled from a large pot that stood simmering on a stove. It was accompanied by a large pile of fresh baked crusty bread rolls.

Brenner spooned some soup into his mouth. It was thick and unctuous. Spicy and full of flavor. 'Man,' he said to Griff. 'This is spectacular.'

Griff nodded as he ate like a starving man, ripping off chunks of bread roll and dipping it in the soup and chasing it with a swig of beer.

The two of them finished their soup in record time and Brenner ordered another brace of beers. He looked around and noticed most of the other patrons were smoking so he assumed either Mexico hadn't instituted a smoking ban or, more likely, that this particular bar thumbed their noses at such pettiness. So he took a pack of Lucky Strike out, lit two and passed one to Griff. The barman slid an ashtray over to them and carried on smearing his filthy cloth over his drinking glasses.

Brenner was halfway through his cigarette when the swing doors burst open and a group of newcomers walked in. Cast from a similar mold to the rest of the patrons, they were of medium height, rangy, weather-beaten, and dressed in worn clothes.

But where the men already in the bar were relaxed, these men were hyped up. Men looking for a mission. And when they saw the two strangers sitting at the bar their mission became apparent. Cause shit with the gringos.

Griff took one look at them and sighed. 'Here comes trouble,' he said as he shook his head. 'Man, what is it with you, Ded?' he asked. 'You attract trouble like shit attracts flies. It's like you're some sort of nutcase magnet.'

Brenner shrugged. 'I honestly don't know,' he admitted. 'It's a curse. Maybe they sense the wolf and have to challenge the Alpha.'

'Whatever,' said Griff. 'You take care of this. I'm too relaxed to give a crap.'

The lead newcomer sauntered over to them, a ready sneer on his face. Behind him, his five cohorts formed a V, three on one side and two on the other.

'You people aren't welcome here,' he said.

'Look, dude,' answered Brenner. 'I'm just not in the mood for this. So, let me paint you a vista. This can go down in one of two ways, you turn around and leave right now. Or I get up and smack you all around for a while, then you leave. If you're still capable of moving, which is less than likely.'

The man laughed. 'Really? The two of you against the five of us? I think maybe you've got it wrong. Tell you what, you leave some money on the counter so my friends and I can have a few drinks then you leave. Now.'

Hey,' interjected Griff. 'Not the two of us, I'm too relaxed to get involved. I already told him. He's on his own. Leave me well out of this.'

'So,' sneered the troublemaker. 'Not only are you old, but you are also a coward.'

Griff shrugged. 'I am what I am, boy. But a coward I am not.'

'Time is up,' said Brenner. 'Banter is over. Leave now or face the consequences.'

'Don't kill anyone,' said Griff.

Brenner exploded into motion.

It wasn't a fight. It was a simply series of movements. A beautifully choreographed sequence of punches and kicks that left the five men lying motionless on the floor.

Brenner had held himself back so, although there was ample evidence of broken limbs, crushed noses and missing teeth, there was very little blood. And none of the broken bones actually penetrated the skin. They were simple fractures, not compound or green twig breaks that would cripple for life.

He hadn't even bothered to take the cigarette out of his mouth.

'Nice job,' said Griff. 'Very restrained.'

'I thought so,' agreed Brenner.

'Unfortunately,' continued Griff. 'The barman seems to disagree.'

Brenner looked up to see the barman had swopped his filthy cloth for a sawn-off, double-barreled shotgun. And it was pointed at Brenner's face.

Brenner held his hands up. 'Whoa. We don't mean any trouble. They started it. I just finished it.'

The barman nodded. 'That's fine,' he said. 'But I think you better leave. You see, Javier and his boys may be a bunch of assholes, but I know them. You, not so much.'

'Fair enough,' admitted Brenner as he threw a pile of dollars down to pay for their food and drink.

The barman motioned them to the door with the shotgun.

'Come on, Griff,' said Brenner. 'Time to move on.'

As he turned to the door Brenner's hand whipped out, faster than a striking rattlesnake, and the next second he was holding the shotgun. He stared at the barmen then grabbed the weapon by the barrel and the butt and slowly bent it into a U shape before he handed it back.

'My friend,' he said. 'A word of advice. We probably won't ever meet again, but if we do, and you point a weapon at me again. You will not live to see the sun set. *Comprende?*'

The barman nodded, his eyes wide open with fear. '*Si*. I understand.'

Griff walked out first and Brenner followed.

The rest of the patrons didn't move.

'You know,' said Griff. 'I can't take you anywhere.'

Brenner laughed. 'Yeah, not exactly the belle of the ball, am I?'

'Look at that,' said Griff as he pointed at one of the vehicles parked outside the bar. 'That must be what Javier arrived in.'

'So what?' said Brenner.

'So, I'll tell you what. It's a Cadillac Escalade ESV. Just shy of one hundred thousand dollars.'

'Yeah, very nice, whatever,' said Brenner. 'I'm not really a car guy.'

Griff shook his head. 'Doesn't it make you wonder what a small-town deadbeat does to drive a big fancy, hundred K automobile. Doesn't it make you in the slightest bit curious?'

'Not really, no,' admitted Brenner. 'Ten to one he's a drug dealer. Look, Griff, we got trouble to spare, let's not look for more.'

'Didn't look like a drug dealer,' argued Griff. 'Not enough bling.'

'He's a dealer,' insisted Brenner. 'I bet if you looked at his SUV you'd find proof.'

'Okay, bet's on,' said Griff. Let's take a look.' He walked over to the SUV, took his revolver out of his belt, reversed it, and smashed the passenger window and reached in to open the door.

'Shit, Griff,' yelled Brenner. 'Have you lost your marbles?'

'Don't sweat it,' said Griff. 'It's not like Javier is going to complain. I mean, what's a broken window compared to the broken bones that you dealt him?'

Brenner shook his head but didn't argue.

Griff took a large leather briefcase from the back seat, put it on the hood and flicked the catches to open it. 'So,' he said. 'You're bet is this will contain drugs?'

Chock full, more than likely,' agreed Brenner.

Griff opened the case.

It was full of documents. Small blue books. Maybe two hundred of them. On the front of each one, the Great Seal of the United States, underneath, the printed words, United States of America.

Griff opened one. It had a name but no photo. He opened another, and another. All had names but no identifying photographs.

Brenner walked over. 'Man, are those fake?'

Griff shrugged. 'I'm not expert enough to know. But they don't look real. Here, look at the quality of the paper. It's not right.'

'Why the hell would someone need so many fake passports?' asked Brenner.

Griff thought for a moment then his expression became thunderous. 'He's a fucking coyotaje.'

'Okay,' said Brenner. 'And what is a coyotaje when it's at home.'

'Scum of the earth,' said Griff. 'People movers. If you want to escape from Mexico to America you pay a coyotaje and he organizes so-called safe passage for you. The bigger operations will also supply fake passports, papers, accommodation. All paid for up front, of course. I hate them.'

'Man,' said Brenner. 'That's a helluva reaction. Didn't know you felt so strongly about the Mexicans coming across the border.'

Griff scowled at Brenner. 'Fuck off, Ded. I couldn't give

a shit about that. I know some of the dudes who come across are bad mothers. Drug dealers, criminals. But the majority I've ever met, and I come across many in my transient type lifestyle, are just poor fuckers who need a break. Families, youngsters looking for work. The way I see it, you must be having a pretty shit life to attempt a border crossing into a country where you don't know anyone and there's a good chance you'll just be sent back.

'Then these coyotaje rip them off. They charge around one thousand bucks per person and the big groups can move up to five hundred people a day. That's big money.

'The sick part is, they take the money up front then seldom deliver on their end of the bargain. The people are abandoned just before the border, or just after. The girls are often raped, the young men beaten up. Fucking sick, man. Scum, like I said.'

Before Brenner could answer another Cadillac Escalade drove up at speed, slew to a stop, and disgorged its passengers. Four hard-looking men made from the same mold as Javier from the bar. But these men were carrying weapons. Sawn-off double-barreled shotguns, twelve gage with pistol grips. Only two shots each but it was more than enough at the range they were standing.

'Great,' said Brenner. 'Here comes a heap of crap. This is all we need.'

'Hands up, gringos,' commanded the one newcomer. 'You really thought you would get away with attacking Javier, then breaking in to his car to steal his papers? Who you working for?'

'You know, I'm getting that question a lot lately,' observed Griff. 'Why can't anyone accept that some people are entrepreneurs who work for themselves?'

'People assume a lack of initiative,' said Brenner. 'Personally, I blame MTV.'

'Yeah,' said Griff. 'But you blame MTV for everything that goes wrong.'

'It's because they don't play enough sixties music. Everything after the sixties was crap.'

'What the fuck are you talking about?' screamed the newcomer. 'I said hands up.'

'Should we kill them all now?' asked Griff.

Brenner shook his head. 'If these dudes are half as shitty as you claim, let's see what happens next. With any luck they'll take us back to their headquarters to have some fun with us. Then we can take the whole organization out.'

'You sure?' asked Griff.

Brenner nodded. 'Sometimes you gotta do what you gotta do.'

The two of them held up their hands.

15

The head of the operation was a Mexican by the name of Francisco Zambrana, or Mister Zee as he was widely known.

Both Griff and Brenner were on their knees in front of the head man, their arms secured behind their backs with zip ties.

Griff's nose was bleeding.

They had struck Brenner numerous times as well but the only result was a small, already healed, cut under his right eye.

Four men stood around them, weapons holstered.

Mister Zee walked up and calmly kicked Brenner in the chest. It was a full-blooded blow. Like a Dallas Cowboy taking a field goal.

He might as well have kicked the wall.

'*Hijo de tu puta madre,*' shouted the gangster as he grabbed his booted foot, staggering back to his chair, and falling into it. 'What the fuck?' He beckoned to his henchmen. 'Teach that *mammon* cocksucker a lesson.'

The four men stepped forward and started whaling on Brenner, fists striking his face, boots raining down on him as they stamped and kicked.

'Enough,' shouted Griff. 'Time to stop this before these dudes start on me.'

Brenner nodded then exploded into his Wolfman form,

shredding his clothes, and sundering the zip ties as he did so. And there was no question as to collateral damage. Anyone in the room was the enemy. Claws slashed, teeth tore and ripped. Blood sprayed.

The four attackers died within seconds and Brenner used his claws to cut Griff's restraints before he grabbed Mister Zee by the throat and lifted him three feet off the ground.

'Please,' gasped Mister Zee. 'I have money. Lots of money. It's yours if you let me live.'

'It's ours anyway,' pointed out Griff as he picked up one of the fallen men's pistols.

'No,' croaked Zee. 'It's in my safe and only I know the combination.'

'Where is the safe,' asked Griff. 'And be quick about the answer or Brenner here may just squeeze your head off.'

'It's behind the painting of me on a horse.'

Griff laughed. 'Original.' He walked over and ripped the painting off the wall to expose the safe. 'Ded, drop the dude and open the safe, I'll keep a bead on him.'

Brenner dropped Zee while Griff trained his pistol on him. The Wolfman walked over to the safe, grabbed the handle and pulled. There was a sound of metal being bent and tortured and the door collapsed and pulled off. Brenner dropped it and scooped out a few plastic wrapped blocks of dollars.

'You'll never get out alive,' shouted Zee. 'I have at least twenty armed guards out there. Leave now and I'll let you live.'

'You may have twenty armed guards,' admitted Griff. 'But I have a werewolf.'

'I'm not a werewolf,' snapped Brenner.

Griff shook his head. 'Really? You wanna go there now. Ruining my perfect one-liner. Shit, man.'

'Sorry,' growled the Wolfman.

'No sense of timing,' complained Griff.

'You're both dead,' screamed Zee.

'No,' answered Griff. 'You are.' He lined up the pistol and shot Zee in the head twice. A perfect double-tap.

Brenner growled.

'What?' asked Griff.

'You shot him,' stated the Wolfman.

'So? What should I have done? Waited for you to eat him?'

'I don't eat people,' said Brenner, his words short and harsh due to the fact they were coming out of a mouth more suited to biting than talking.

Griff raised an eyebrow.

Brenner looked away. 'Okay, I hardly ever eat people. Let's get out of here, we'll do as much damage as we can on the way out.'

'Hold on,' said Griff as he grabbed a briefcase from Mister Zee's desk. He opened the catches and chucked the paperwork on the floor. Then he crammed in as much money as he could. 'Not sure but I reckon that's around four hundred K. Not a bad day's work.'

'That's not why we're here,' said Brenner.

'I know. But it doesn't do any harm. Bear in mind The Pastor's boys trashed my Winnebago. I'm homeless and without computers. This will go a long way to getting me back on the road.'

The sound of approaching, running footsteps reached then as Mister Zee's men ran toward the sound of the gunshots.

'Here they come,' said Brenner. 'I'm going to take the fight to them. Better if I take them all out. I ruined my clothes when I changed and I would like some time to see if I can get a new set. Someone here must be around my size.'

'Go get them, Ded,' said Griff. 'I'm right behind you.'

Brenner waited until he could hear them just outside the door then he kicked out, smashing it off its hinges and into the corridor. It hammered into the group of men outside, hitting them like a runaway train. Out of the five who'd arrived only two survived and they were both badly injured. Brenner leapt over them, leaving Griff to finish them off.

Brenner jumped from the top of the sweeping staircase to the bottom in one bound, landing amongst the next group of bandits who were rushing to their master's assistance. Again he worked fast and messy. Everyone here was bad. Everyone was the enemy.

Limbs were removed, necks broken, skulls crushed. No one even got a shot off.

Griff followed behind, the odd crack of his pistol the only sign some had been left alive, if only barely.

Brenner had not heard of coyotajes before but the mere

fact the strong were preying on the weak churned his stomach and his anger was righteous and fulsome.

Retribution.

As he ran out of the front door he took his first hits. High up on his chest. Something large. Most likely a 5.56mm round. An assault rifle. The massive energy the round imparted threw Brenner off his feet and blood sprayed high. Shotguns and handguns weren't a problem. But modern hyper-velocity rounds took their toll. As he rolled to his feet he knew his right arm would be useless to him for the next ten minutes or so.

For a major gunshot wound to heal in a matter of minutes is nothing short of miraculous.

But ten *seconds* in mortal combat is an eternity. Let alone ten whole minutes.

So he morphed to full wolf mode.

With only one arm Brenner knew he was not running at his full deadly Wolfman capacity. But he knew he could move almost as well on three legs as on four, and now his jaws were his most powerful asset, almost nullifying the wounded arm.

He leapt high and landed on the gunman with the assault rifle, grasping the top of his skull in his massive jaws and neatly slicing the top off like a boiled egg at a breakfast table.

Again he leapt, spun, bit, ripped. In the background the muted pop of Griff's weapon punctuated the ballet of combat like a tympani.

And it was over.

Less than a minute had passed since Brenner had smashed the door down. Less than sixty seconds.

And twenty-three men had died.

One every two and a half seconds.

Evil had been punished.

Griff picked up the discarded assault rifle, checked the mag and slipped the safety on. He touched Brennerwolf on his wounded shoulder. 'You gonna be okay?'

The wolf whined and nodded.

Griff knew Brenner would stay in wolf mode until the wound healed. His recovery processes worked much faster when he was full animal.

Brennerwolf cocked his head to one side, then he pushed his nose against Griff and set off at a trot around the huge house.

Griff followed, slipping the safety catch off the assault rifle and carrying it at high port, ready to rock and roll. He had used one of the spare zip ties to attach the briefcase full of money to his belt. There was no way he was letting it out of his sight.

As they rounded the corner they saw two Mercedes L-series trucks, their backs covered in canvas. Milling around the trucks were at least a hundred people. Men and women, mainly young. Teenagers to midtwenties. They saw the wolf and backed away, some voicing cries of fear.

Griff held his hand up. 'We mean no harm,' he said. 'Is anyone here in charge?'

One of the young men stepped forward. 'My name is Miguel,' he said. 'I am the spokesperson for the group. May I ask what is happening? We have heard many gunshots and our drivers rushed off. Who are you? What is that?' he pointed at Brennerwolf.

'My name is Griff. That is a wolf. He's friendly. Sort of.'

Miguel shook his head. 'That is no wolf. I have seen many wolves but never one the size of a horse.'

'Well, you can't say that anymore,' quipped Griff. 'So, I take it you lot are here to be escorted across the border?'

Miguel nodded.

'Sorry about that,' said Griff. 'But the coyotajes are all dead. There'll be no cross-border trips today. You all need to go home.'

'You killed them?' asked Miguel.

Griff nodded.

'But we have all already paid. Now what do we do. You have stolen our money from us. You have taken away our chance to go to America. To freedom. Why did you do this? Are you a rival gang?'

'No,' said Griff. 'We did it because they were evil men. They deserved no less than they got. Retribution for the terrible things they have done. The rapes, the killing.'

Miguel shook his head. 'Some of our families saved for many years to send us across the border. Now you and your wolf that is not a wolf have ruined everything for us.' He turned to face the crowd of people which was now starting to draw closer, their anger starting to outweigh their fear.

'*Ellos han matado a los coyotajes*,' shouted Miguel to the crowd. 'They have killed the coyotajes. Now we have nowhere to go. They have taken our freedom.'

Griff shook his head. 'Really? You, stupid fuck. They would have raped most of these girls. They may even have killed some of you. I saw the passports they had for you. They wouldn't even stand up to the slightest scrutiny. You were all being ripped off.'

'We know these things,' countered Miguel. 'The girls are all told to go onto birth control pills before they make a trip such as this. We accept the fact some of us may die. All these things we accept. But we do not accept an old man and his pet killing our only chance at freedom.'

The crowd surged forward, some shouting, others with murderous intent in their eyes.

Brenner morphed into Wolfman mode.

Then he threw back his head and howled.

The crowd fell over each other as they ran to escape.

'Stop,' growled Brenner at the top of his voice. The combination of the howl combined with the command halted the crowd like they had been frozen. Terror had made them puppets to Brenner's will.

He walked around them, like a sheepdog corralling its flock. For the main they kept their eyes down. Averted. Hands clutched together. Waiting for the inevitable.

'You are all mistaken,' growled Brenner Wolfman. 'We have not taken your freedom. We have granted you freedom. The only problem is, we have granted you freedom to do what you do not want to do. You are free to stay here. You are free to make this country better. You are free to not get raped or killed crossing the border.

'But I am aware of your problems. After all, there must be a reason almost fifty thousand of you try to cross the border every month. And I know most of you will work hard and do your best.

'It's not for me to argue the morality of what you all want to do. Frankly, I couldn't give a shit whether you stay here or try to cross over to America. But you don't need the coyotajes. You don't need murdering scum to help you. The reason Griff and I killed Mister Zee and his people is because we saw an evil. An evil that needed to be exterminated. It had nothing to do with your wanting to cross the border.'

Brenner Wolfman turned to Griff.

'Give them the money.'

Griff went pale. 'Come on, Ded. That's our money. How the hell am I ever gonna afford a new Winnebago?'

'Griff, hand it over. A lot of it is probably theirs at any rate.'

Griff pulled out a knife and cut the zip tie connecting the briefcase to his belt. Then he held the case out to Miguel.

The Mexican took it with a puzzled look on his face.

'Open it,' said Brenner.

He did and a smile lit up his features.

'Share it amongst everyone. Fairly,' continued Brenner. 'Take whatever else you want from this place, trucks, anything. Turn this place into a refuge if you want. But remember, you are now free to do as you want. Don't fuck up this chance.'

Miguel bowed low. 'I thank you, wolf devil.'

Griff sniggered. 'Devil,' he muttered. 'These dicks are just gonna take the money and pay some other bunch of thugs to take them across the border. Fucking waste of cash.'

Brenner said nothing as he stalked back to the house, looking for a bedroom that would hopefully have some clothes that fit him.

Half an hour later they were driving again. Brenner sat in the passenger seat. He wore jeans that were slightly too short, but the lack of length wasn't too apparent as he had found a pair of cowboy boots which fit perfectly. His shirt was also a little too tight and he had rolled the sleeves up to disguise the fact that the cuffs only reached to the middle of his forearms.

Griff drove without speaking, still irritated at how Brenner had made him give away their cash windfall.

'There's always more money,' said Brenner. 'Don't sweat it.'

'Yeah,' said Griff. 'It's fine for you to say, you haven't lost your home'

'True,' admitted Brenner. 'But then I haven't had a permanent place to rest my head since the sixties.'

Griff sighed and shook his head, there wasn't much he could say about that.

16

They came across the hospital about five miles beyond the tiny enclave of Los Juguetes, and parked up in the brush a mile away to do a visual recce of the place.

Four identical single-story buildings in a row, all linked by prefabricated corridors. Flat roofs, unadorned concrete walls, small, barred windows, and blacktop parking areas.

The one building stood out from the rest in that it had a tall concrete chimney next to it. Smoke drifted from the opening. Obviously, some sort of incineration plant for medical waste.

The whole center was surrounded by a ten-foot-high, chain-link fence. Unsurprisingly, armed guards patrolling the perimeter.

A discreet sign read, *Transatlantic Medical Research Center.*

There were large floodlights at even intervals along the fence and in the corners of each building.

It would be impossible to approach the place and remain unseen. Even at night.

'This is not going to be easy,' said Griff. 'Gonna call for a little more subtlety than you're used to.'

'Hey,' said Brenner. 'I don't always just go wolf and attack, I can do subtle.'

'Oh, yeah?'

Brenner thought for a few seconds. 'OK not so much,' he admitted. 'But I am open to suggestions.'

'We have a few problems,' said Griff. 'Firstly, a full-on assault will bring down a world of hurt on us. Those guards are packing assault rifles. Secondly, we don't even know if this is the right place. Thirdly, we have no idea who is innocent and who is a slicing and dicing Frankenstein doctor. For all we know, this place could be doing legitimate research and only a couple of bad apples do the illegal organ thing on the side.'

'I get it,' said Brenner. 'Suggestions?'

'Not much we can do. Our options are pretty limited,' answered Griff. 'All I can think of is for us to stake the place out and wait for someone to leave. There's a bunch of cars parked there which leads me to believe the staff must leave the place every now and then. I would guess one of those buildings is living quarters because there's fuck all around here where staff could live, but they must go out for R&R or a change of scenery every now and then.'

'We aren't exactly kitted up for a stakeout,' noted Brenner.

'We got water,' counted Griff. 'Got cigarettes. A few candy bars. We'll live, as long as it doesn't stretch to more than a couple of days.'

'So when they come out, we follow them. Then what?' asked Brenner.

'Take them somewhere where we won't attract attention and question them. Simple.'

'If they're innocent? Then what do we do with them?'

Griff shrugged. 'Cross that bridge when we get to it,' he

answered. 'No point in wishing trouble for ourselves before we find it.'

Brenner nodded his agreement and the two of them leaned back against the side of the Range Rover and started their long boring vigil.

Eventually the sun set. They waited until eleven o'clock at night then Brenner told Griff to catch a nap. He would wake him if anything happened or, if not, in a couple hours to do his shift.

The sun rose the next morning at a little after five o'clock. Brenner hadn't woken Griff, choosing to let the physically older man get some rest.

Because, although Brenner was actually almost exactly the same age, he still looked twenty-five and he found he didn't need nearly as much sleep as a normal human, often going for days with only a couple of hours of downtime.

Griff climbed out of the Range Rover, stretched, and rubbed his eyes. 'Anything happen?'

Brenner shook his head. 'No. And I'm sure nothing will happen for a couple more hours. They're all still asleep, I would guess. You keep an eye out, I'm going to take a stroll.'

'Why?' asked Griff.

'Don't feel like candy for breakfast. Going to see if I can rustle up anything else.'

As Brenner spoke he was stripping, folding his clothes, and putting them on the hood of the SUV. Then he morphed into wolf mode and ran off.

Griff lit a cigarette and kept an eye on the medical research center.

Half an hour later, Brenner walked up in human form. In his right hand he held three dead Jack Rabbits. He dumped them on the ground and got dressed. Then he used the tire iron to dig a fire pit, ensuring the SUV was between the facility and the pit. He collected some dry brush and wood, used his knife to whittle some wood shavings off a twig and started a small smokeless fire in the pit. Then he quickly dressed the rabbits, spitted them and laid them over the fire pit, turning them every few minutes.

They cooked in under half an hour and he let the fire die down, leaving the rabbits to cool for twenty minutes before he offered one to Griff.

'Needs salt,' said Griff in between mouthfuls.

'Yeah,' agreed Brenner. 'And a side of steak. And potatoes and gravy. And room service.'

'Point taken,' admitted Griff. 'Better than candy for breakfast. Thanks, dude.'

'No problem.'

When they had eaten, Brenner threw the carcasses into the fire pit and filled it in. Then the two men lit up and smoked in companionable silence for a while.

Finally, just after midday, a car approached the gates. A guard opened up and the car proceeded along the road toward Los Juguetes.

The two men clambered into the SUV and followed, keeping well back, confident there was no way to lose their prey, as there was only a single road in and out of the whole area.

They followed the car for about three miles, until it was out of sight of the medical facility, then the driver pulled off the road and stopped.

'Do you think they've seen us,' said Griff.

'Maybe. But even if they had, why stop, and pull over,' answered Brenner as he also pulled over so they could observe what was happening.

The driver got out of the car and walked a few yards away from the road. Even from the distance Griff and Brenner were watching from it was immediately apparent that the driver was female.

Long dark hair, trim figure, court shoes.

She was clutching something small in her right hand, holding it up toward the sky then bringing it down to glance at it before walking a few more steps and repeating the ritual.

'What the hell is she doing?' asked Griff. 'Is it some sort of light detector? Is she checking for radiation?'

Brenner pulled his cell phone out of his trouser pocket and checked it. 'No signal,' he said. 'She's checking for cell phone coverage. Probably doesn't get any at the facility and she wants to make a call. Obviously, there's a spot out here that picks up signal.'

'They gotta have landlines at the facility. Or if not, then a satellite uplink. She doesn't need to drive all the way out here and stumble around in the brush to make a call,' observed Griff.

'Unless she wants to make a private call,' said Brenner. 'I reckon we need to have a chat to Miss private caller. See what she's hiding from her employers.'

They got back into the car and drove along the road, taking care not to drive too fast as to appear threatening nor so slowly as to attract attention.

When they were next to the girl's car, Brenner pulled in front of it, switched off and got out, followed closely by Griff.

The girl didn't notice them for a few seconds and when she did she went pale and her hand flew to her mouth as she stifled a surprised gasp.

But she recovered quickly, set her shoulders, and walked confidently toward them. 'Good morning,' she greeted them. 'How can I help? I assume Doctor Wegner sent you.'

Neither Griff nor Brenner answered, using the age-old interrogation technique of saying nothing and letting the interviewee fill the gaps.

They all stared at each other for a good ten seconds and the girl cracked first. 'Look, I was just going for a drive to clear my head and saw there was some cell phone signal. Thought I'd make a call. It's not against the law, you know.'

Still the two men did not speak.

'Oh, fuck you,' snapped the girl as she walked to her car.

Brenner stood in her way. 'Sorry ma'am, he said. 'But we have a few questions, if you don't mind.'

'Actually,' she replied. 'I do mind. I have already

expressed my misgivings to Doctor Wegner. And I must say this is typical of him to send two bully boys along to intimidate me. Well, let me tell you something, it takes more than a mentally deficient jock and a creepy old man to put the fear into me. So you can both just fuck off and leave me alone.'

Brenner tried unsuccessfully to stifle a laugh as Griff did a perfect double take.

'Creepy old man,' he said. 'I'm barely over seventy-five,' he objected. 'That's not old. And as for creepy, well that's just patently untrue.'

Brenner shrugged. 'What can I say?' he noted. 'The girl tells it like it is.'

'Hey, at least I'm not mentally deficient,' said Griff.

'She just doesn't know me yet,' argued Brenner. 'Give her time, she'll realize her mistake.'

'You guys aren't from the research laboratory,' noted the girl.

'What gave us away?' asked Griff.

'Not sure,' she admitted. 'Probably the fact you seem to have a modicum of humor. And you didn't start to threaten me straight away. So, who are you?'

'I'm Reece Griffin and this is Brenner. And you are?'

'Materia Santiago. My friends call me Matty.'

Griff held his hand out. 'My friends call me Griff.' He nodded toward Brenner. 'He doesn't have any friends. Except for me. Call him Brenner, or Ded if you want. He answers to both.'

Matty shook Griff's hand, then Brenner's. 'Okay,' she said. 'If you aren't from the Research Lab, where are you from and what are you doing here?'

'First, we need you to answer some questions,' said Brenner. 'Like, why the surreptitious phones call? Surely if you wanted to call someone you got landlines at the facility?'

Matty shook her head. 'I can't go there.'

'Sorry, Matty,' said Griff. 'But you have to. Please don't mistake our politeness for weakness. We have things to do and we are going to do them. And right now we don't have any idea what side you're on, so you better start talking.'

Again she shook her head.

Griff sighed. 'Look, if it helps, we have nothing to do with the facility. In fact, we're here on what you could call a mission. Now, I'm not saying we are American Government officials ... but then I'm not saying we aren't. So any truthful answers from you could be a great help. For example, what the hell is going on at that research center?'

Matty licked her lips nervously before she spoke. 'I got my medical degree at the *Universidad Nacional Autónoma de México,* then I went on to specialize in research, particularly gene therapy and human genetic engineering. Because I didn't study at any of the more fashionable universities I struggled to get a research placement. Eventually, after a couple of years of searching, I was approached by Doctor Wegner on behalf of the *Transatlantic Medical Research Group.* Although I had never met Doctor Wegner personally, I was well aware of his work in gene mutations and its effect on organ rejection in patients.

'Obviously, I jumped at the chance to work with him, even though it was in the middle of nowhere.

'That was six months ago and since then I have started to have some reservations.'

'Like what?' asked Brenner.

'I think he may be conducting illegal experiments. And before you ask what, I honestly have no idea. All I know is. People arrive at building four but I never see them leave. In fact, I'm pretty sure I was never even meant to see them arrive. They come between three and four in the morning. Hustled in without lights or talking and that's it.

'I can't check on them because building four is out of bounds unless you have a triple A card, access all areas. I don't. And the only reason I saw them is because I have trouble sleeping and I'm often awake at those hours.

'Look, I could be wrong. There is a helicopter, an Airbus, it makes at least one, sometimes two trips a day. Maybe they smuggle the people out in that, but I haven't seen anyone so that's unlikely. They must be keeping them in building four. That's why I suspect Doctor Wegner is doing some sort of research on them. And the whole cloak-and-dagger routine makes me suspect it's probably illegal. Or at least, morally suspect.'

'So the phone call?' asked Griff again.

'I was going to contact an old friend,' answered Matty. 'One of my professors from the university. He knows a lot of people, and I was going to ask him if he had heard of any research Wegner was doing. Rumors, that sort of thing.'

Griff sighed and turned to Brenner. 'You tell her.'

'Why me?'

Griff shrugged. 'Because she's not going to believe you then I can back you up with a cogent and logical explanation. Gives us two shots at the target.'

Matty raised an eyebrow. 'Guys. I'm right here. Talk to me, not about me.'

'Okay,' said Brenner. 'We got good news and bad news. The good news is, you're right, the doctor is doing some seriously illegal shit.'

'I knew it,' interjected Matty. 'Probably drug tests.'

Brenner shook his head. 'No, this is the bad news. He's actually harvesting organs.'

Matty stared at the big man for a few seconds then she shook her head. 'No way. I don't believe you.'

Griff snorted. 'Told you.'

'You mean he's buying kidneys, parts of the liver, then selling them on?'

'No,' answered Brenner. 'He's taking it all. Hearts, lungs, blood, skin, kidneys, liver. The whole thing. Harvesting the lot.'

Matty went pale. 'That's murder. No,' she denied once again. 'He's a doctor. There's no way he would do that.'

'Listen, Matty,' said Griff. 'We've come here directly from the farms where these people were kept. Under armed guards, enforced labor and controlled diets. Then when there's a call they get transported here and Wegner slices and dices them. The Airbus helicopter obviously takes the organs to the end users. Not sure how they dispose of the leftovers.'

'The incinerator,' whispered Matty. 'It goes all day. I've often wondered why there was so much organic waste being burned. Now it makes sense.'

'You believe us?' asked Griff.

'It's unbelievable,' said Matty. 'But I do believe. At least enough to not totally reject your premise.'

'So will you help us?' asked Brenner.

'How?'

'We need to get in to the facility. Take a look at this building four. If Wegner is doing what we think, then we take our next step after that.'

'And what would your next step be?' asked Matty. 'Call the authorities?'

'Think we'd have much joy calling the *Federales*. The local Mexican cops?'

Matty shook her head. 'No. They're notorious for, well, being pretty ineffective as well as being open to bribery and corruption. We'd have to go a lot higher.'

'Like what?' asked Brenner.

Matty stared for a while then shook her head again. 'I don't know.'

'Well, don't worry about it,' said Griff. 'Brenner and I will take the next step. And believe me, Doctor Wegner won't be slicing and dicing after that.'

'I cannot condone vigilantism,' warned Matty.

'Condone it, don't condone it,' said Brenner. 'Doesn't matter. We do what we do, your approval is not necessary.'

'Who are you people?' asked Matty.

Brenner looked at her and his golden eyes crackled with restrained power. 'We are vengeance,' he answered.

The girl thought for a moment longer then nodded. 'Okay. What do you want me to do?'

'Hide Brenner in your trunk,' said Griff. 'Would it work or do they search the vehicle every time?'

'It would work,' said Matty. 'They're actually pretty slack. As long as they know you. If they don't, they get all gung ho and official. But I must warn you, there are at least twenty guards and they are all armed. I assume that is going to be a problem.'

Griff shrugged. 'That's their problem, not ours. I'll ask Brenner to be as gentle as he can be. But I can't guarantee anything. There may very well be bloodshed, depending on how pissed off he gets.'

'Are you being serious?' asked Matty. 'Twenty armed men and you make jokes about it?'

'Who's joking?' asked Griff.

And Matty saw that neither the old man nor Brenner had cracked even a glimpse of a smile.

'Okay,' she conceded as she used her remote to open the trunk. 'Get in.'

Brenner climbed into the truck, curling up so as to fit in. 'When you park, as you leave, please make sure you crack the trunk open. I'll hold it shut from the inside but I need to get out easily.'

'They'll see you almost straight away,' observed Matty.

'I'll wait until night,' answered Brenner.

'All day?'

'Yep. It's not a problem. I've spent much longer in much worse places.'

'There's still a full contingent of guards at night,' warned Matty. 'There's still a good chance they'll see you.'

'They won't,' said Brenner.

'They might.'

'Trust me,' answered Brenner. 'No one sees me at night when I don't want to be seen.'

'I'll get as close as I safely can,' said Griff. 'Provide some emergency cover with the 30-06. Be safe.'

'You too, old friend,' said Brenner.

Matty closed the lid, got into the driver's seat, and headed back to the facility.

17

Brenner couldn't sleep for fear of the trunk lid closing on him. He knew he could still get out of the car, but smashing open the trunk wasn't the best way to remain unseen.

He waited until the sun had been below the horizon for a good four hours before he slowly pushed the lid up and rolled out.

Blending with the shadows he moved to the row of buildings. Every now and then he would stop, cock his head to one side and sniff the air, allowing his senses of smell and hearing to detect any approaching guards.

He moved around the first building, peering into any windows he could. There was little of interest. Empty offices. The odd one with someone still at their desk, burning the night oil. A couple of small laboratories. A storage room full of nondescript cardboard boxes.

A pair of guards came walking around the corner and Brenner literally melted into the darkness. Six feet four inches and over two hundred thirty pounds of person just disappeared as he became one with the shadows.

He waited until he could no longer see them and continued his recce.

The second building was obviously the living and recreational area. There were more windows and they were smaller. Many had drapes drawn across them, but the ones he could see through revealed sparsely furnished rooms with single beds and cheap wardrobes, small two seat tables.

Further on he saw a well-equipped commercial kitchen and a common room of some sort. Refectory style tables at the one end, a couple of pool tables, lounge seats, and a large TV at the other. The walls painted in various shades of depression. Greens and browns.

Asylum chic.

Soulless, institutional, and depressing.

It reminded Brenner of a minimum-security prison, complete with the fencing and the guards, and he wondered how anyone could work here voluntarily.

The third building contained more offices and laboratories.

But the fourth building was different. Internally barred windows with heavy drapes drawn across. The two access doors were steel sheathed and double locked.

Brenner couldn't see anything of interest.

There was a third entrance, via building three through a prefabricated corridor. Brenner figured, if he wanted to get in then that was the way to go.

He needed to find Matty. Keeping all senses alert for the patrolling guards he went back to building number two and moved from window to window, pausing to sniff the air, searching for Matty's scent. When he passed by the last window on the right-hand side of the building he knew it was her room and he peeked into the window. The room was dark and no one was in. He grabbed the bottom of the window, pulled it open and climbed inside, closing it behind him.

Then he sat on the bed and waited.

An hour later the door opened and Matty walked in, closing it behind her. She started to undress without turning the light on, relying on the faint moon outside. As she pulled off her blouse, Brenner spoke, trying to keep his voice low and unthreatening.

'Matty,' he said. 'It's me, Brenner.'

'Holy shit,' she exclaimed as she picked up her blouse and held it in front of her. 'What the hell? You scared the crap out of me.' To Brenner's disappointment, she yanked her blouse back on. 'How did you get in?'

'Window.'

'But the place is crawling with guards.'

Brenner shrugged. 'They didn't see me.'

'What are you doing here?'

'I need to get into building four. The exterior doors are solid steel. I could probably break them down but it would attract unwanted attention, so I figured I'd try to get in through the connecting corridor.'

Matty snorted. 'You reckon you could smash those steel doors down?'

Brenner nodded. 'Would make too much noise. Hopefully this way will be quieter.'

Matty stared for a moment before she spoke. 'My God, you're serious, aren't you?'

'Why would I lie?' asked Brenner.

Matty thought for a while as she contemplated the big

man sitting on her bed. 'You are one strange man, Brenner,' she said. 'But for some reason, I trust you. Right, how do you want this to go down?'

'When is the best time to sneak unseen through the corridors?'

'Few more hours,' answered Matty. 'Four o'clock or so. 'Everyone's asleep then. I'll show you the way, we can use my pass, but that'll only get us to the last door. Then you'll have to do your smash-hulk thing unless you can think of a cleverer way to get through the door. It's just like the others. Solid steel.'

'We'll cross that bridge when we come to it,' said Brenner. 'Now, I need a rest. Trapped in the car trunk all day did my back no favors.'

'You want a shower?' asked Matty. 'A blast of hot water will do wonders for cramped muscles.'

Brenner nodded. 'Thanks.'

Matty opened the door to the en suite. 'Towel's in there. Help yourself.'

The big man indulged himself more than he usually did. The water was hot and the pressure was good, easing the stiffness out of his body. After twenty minutes he turned the shower off.

Matty looked up to see Brenner enter the room with a towel around his waist.

'Sorry, Matty,' he said. 'I turned the bathroom into a bit of a sauna. My clothes are damp from the steam. Wondered if I could hang them over the chair for a while, let them dry out. We've got loads of time before we need to head out.'

'Sure,' answered Matty. 'Hang them there.' She pointed at two chairs gracing a small table. The aircon should get the damp out.

Brenner did so and sat on the edge of the bed again.

Matty stared at him unashamedly, studying the myriad of healed scars on his torso.

Finally she spoke. 'What the hell happened to you?'

Brenner shrugged. 'Been around a bit. Run into some bad dudes.'

Matty walked over, sat next to him, and ran her hand over his chest. It was like touching latex covered concrete. Impossibly hard, yet still tactile. 'There must be over a hundred scars. How did you survive?'

'Fast healer.'

She shook her head as she continued to trace the scars on his skin. 'No,' she said. 'This is strange. The scars are all well-healed, but I can see no sign of surgery. I did my residence in Mexico City. I saw a lot of gunshot wounds, stabbing, that sort of thing. And when the victim recovered there was always a sign of surgery. Stitch marks, staples, debridement. These are untouched. Like they just healed up naturally, which is impossible.'

She ran her fingers over a grouping of six bullet wounds in his chest, then she checked his back. There were six matching exit wounds, larger and more ragged. But once again, fully healed with only the lightest of scarring.

'These should have killed you,' she stated. 'They would

have shredded your heart, lungs, all the vital veins and arteries, not to mention your spine. But you're still here.' Matty frowned as she pointed out more injuries. 'Almost all of these should have been fatal. Or at least left permanent damage. What the hell was this?' She tracked her finger across a long scar reaching from his under his chin at an oblique angle to his hip.

'Car crash. Hit and run driver.'

'Did they catch him?'

Brenner nodded. 'Yes, I did.'

'You did? How long did it take you?'

The big man shrugged. 'Not sure. A couple of minutes. I'm a lot faster than a car, even when injured.'

Matty laughed. 'You're teasing me,' she said. 'Don't. That's mean.' She cocked her fist and slugged Brenner in the shoulder. Immediately regretting it as her fist came into contact with steel-solid muscle.

'Ow!' she yelped, and shook her hand.

Brenner grabbed it. 'Sorry about that,' he said. He raised her hand to his mouth and kissed the knuckles.

Matty was amazed at how soft his lips were compared to the iron-hardness of his body. At how gentle was his touch. The concern in his voice.

'It's fine,' she said. But she didn't pull her hand away.

She looked into his eyes and marveled at the color. Yellow-gold with flecks of black. The pupils hugely dilated. And a strange feeling came over her. A combination of fear and lust. Of need and trepidation. A wave of desire that seemed to come from her very core.

And she blushed with the strength of her longing. It was as if she were obeying some deep seated primal urge. The need to become one with the Alpha male in the room.

The animalistic need to mate.

She leaned forward and kissed Brenner on the lips, grasping his hair as she did so, her tongue hungrily seeking his.

The big man froze momentarily then reacted, mirroring her mood as he put his arms around her.

Matty stood and tore her blouse off, then her trousers.

Brenner stood, letting his towel fall to the floor. Then he lifted her up and laid her on the bed. Reverentially. Gently.

He lay beside her.

Matty's heart caught in her chest as she felt the heat coming off his body in waves. He felt like a furnace. Like a massive piece of machinery running hot and heavy.

A jet engine. Or an Abrahams battle tank.

Their love making was frantic. She took from him and he gave. Willingly.

And after she was spent, her limbs like wet string, her skin flushed like she had been in a sauna, her heart full of emotion, he kissed her again and put his arm around her.

With a smile on her face, Matty fell into a deep, satisfied sleep.

18

Matty led the way, walking softly but with a purpose. The buildings were easy to navigate, basically a central corridor with the rooms leading off it. The two of them proceeded through the living quarters and, using her access card, they went into building number three. It was as quiet as the grave. Dull nightlights glimmered in the corridor. Low energy LED's.

At the end of the corridor was a normal security door leading to the passage that would take them to the steel door preventing any non-authorized person from entering the final building.

'You know what?' asked Brenner. 'Just had a thought. Maybe I should just go and grab Doctor Wegner and ask politely what the hell is going on here.'

Matty smiled. 'Could do, except for the fact that his living quarters are in building four. I don't know anyone who has actually been there but rumor has it no expense has been spared. Absolute luxury.'

'Oh well,' sighed Brenner. 'It was just a thought. Can your card open this door?'

'Yep. But it'll do you no good,' said Matty. 'The door into building four is one of those solid steel affairs. Just like the outside ones.'

'Let's go take a look,' said Brenner.

Matty swiped the card and the lock clicked open. The two

of them strode along the corridor, stopping in front of the steel door.

Brenner placed his hand on it and thought for a while. Then he turned to Matty. 'Perhaps you should leave now,' he said. 'Things are about to get weird. Not to mention dangerous. Whatever happens, if you get caught with me from anytime hereon in, it'll be the end of your career with this corporation.'

'As well hanged for a sheep as a lamb,' quipped Matty. 'I'm in, whatever happens. If what you told me is true then we need to stop Wegner. We need to stop the whole organization.'

'Okay,' agreed Brenner. 'Now I am going to smash this door down, but first I am going to have to change.'

Matty grinned. 'You mean, go all green and grow muscles and start to talk in monosyllables?'

Brenner nodded. 'Sort of. Look, Matty, I'm going to become a being capable of breaking a steel door. I will not harm you. It will still be me, but in a different form. Do you trust me?'

Matty got a worried look on her face. 'Brenner,' she said. 'Please don't tell me you've lost the plot. People don't simply become other things. If we need to back down, now is the time. There is no shame in going back to my room and sneaking you out of the facility. You've done what you can, let's just call it a day. We tried.'

Brenner started to strip his clothes off, starting with his shirt.

'Oh, shit,' exclaimed Matty. 'What are you doing? Stop it, Brenner. Put your clothes back on.'

He stood in front of her. Naked. Standing tall.

Matty shook her head, her expression one of pity. 'Come on, Brenner,' she said softly as she held out her hand. 'Let's go. Everything is going to be okay.'

Then he changed.

A flowing metamorphosis of man to beast. A perfect blend of humanity and brutality. In mere seconds, Brenner had shed the thin veneer of mankind's evolution and replaced it with the synergistic combination of modern intellect and primitive aggression.

Over seven feet tall and four-hundred pounds of barely bridled violence.

Wolfman.

With a single punch, he smashed the steel door off its hinges and into the corridor behind it.

Then he turned to Matty and smiled, exposing his three-inch-long canines and razor-sharp incisors.

'Brenner smash,' he said, his voice more a growl than a human vocalization.

Matty's face drained of blood and she began to sink to the floor as her system shut down from a total overload. Brenner grabbed her before she collapsed, making sure he used the utmost care so as not to crush her flesh and bones.

He lowered her gently and morphed back into human mode.

Matty blinked and stared at Brenner, wide-eyed in shock.

'Brenner?'

He nodded. 'It's still me.'

'You became a werewolf,' whispered Matty.

Brenner shook his head. 'No. Not a werewolf,' he stated. 'I'm the result of a genetic experiment carried out by the United States Army under Project Bloodborn.'

'You became a werewolf,' repeated Matty, her lips quivering with emotion.

Brenner sighed. 'Okay, fine, I became a werewolf, sort of.'

'That's impossible,' whispered Matty.

'Obviously not,' said Brenner as he changed back into human mode and pulled his clothes on. He held out his hand. 'Are you coming?'

Matty nodded and, with his help, stood.

'Do you want to take a look around?' asked Brenner. 'Or should we just go straight to Wegner's rooms and have a chat?'

'I'm surprised he hasn't already raised the alarm,' said Matty. 'That door being smashed off wasn't quiet.'

'You'd be surprised,' said Brenner. 'People simply don't expect loud noises to be things like impenetrable steel doors being knocked off their hinges, or walls being shattered or suchlike. They tend to wait and listen to hear if there's another loud noise and, if not, they normally dismiss it as an unexplained anomaly. Particularly if nothing untoward has ever happened before.'

'Well, in that case,' said Matty. 'Let's find his rooms and speak to him.'

The first thing Brenner noticed was the doors leading off the corridor were locked from the outside. Large, stainless steel padlocks and bolts top and bottom.

At the end of the corridor they came across the first door without a padlock.

'I would hazard a guess this is the doctor's living quarters,' said Brenner. 'Should we knock or just let ourselves in?'

Matty shrugged. 'This is your thing,' she said. 'Do whatever you think is correct. I don't exactly know the accepted protocol here. In fact I'm still trying to get my head around the whole werewolf thing.'

'Project Bloodborn,' mumbled Brenner. 'Not werewolf. I think I'll knock.'

'Are you going to stay human?' asked Matty.

'I'm always human,' quipped Brenner.

'You know what I mean.'

He nodded. 'Yeah, at least to start with. Sometimes you can't question someone after they've seen the beast. Their brain just short circuits and they go all catatonic. Drool and go into shock and shit like that.'

Brenner balled his hand into a fist and hammered on the door like he was trying to raise the dead. He kept it up until the door opened then, as it did, he kicked it hard, slamming it into the man who had opened it and throwing him to the floor.

'That's him,' said Matty. 'Doctor Wegner.'

Brenner grabbed the doctor by his shirt and dragged him

into the apartment. Matty followed.

The residence was the diametric opposite of the living quarters the staff stayed in. Spacious, carpeted with deep pile wool, subtle hidden lighting, original artwork, sumptuous furniture. The sounds of Miles Davis drifted through the rooms via a series of ceiling mounted speakers.

Luxury.

Brenner picked the doctor up and threw him onto one of the leather wingback chairs, then he stood over him and waited for a reaction.

The doctor was a small man. Tiny, even. Maybe five feet, one hundred pounds. His head was disproportionally large for his slight body and his neck was so thin it seemed like it shouldn't support his massive cranium. The left side of his face was covered in a ridged, port-wine stain birthmark that crawled across his face from hairline to neck, reddening his eye in the process.

But when he spoke, Brenner had to stop himself from doing a double take. The doctor's voice was pure velvet. Deep, resonant, and commanding. Completely at odds with his diminutive stature and unappealing appearance.

He utterly ignored Brenner as if he wasn't there and spoke directly to Matty.

'Doctor Santiago,' he said. 'I assume you can explain this invasion of my personal quarters.'

'We have questions, Doctor Wegner,' answered Matty.

'I see. Well I must say this seems to be a rather extreme way of obtaining a few minutes for a question and answer session. I have made it plain to my staff that I am always available to help. I must say I am extremely disappointed in your behavior.'

The words should have sounded trite, like a master lecturing a recalcitrant student. But coming out of his mouth they throbbed with sincerity. His velvet voice added emotion and depth to every word he uttered. *'This man should be in politics,'* thought Brenner. *'His voice is absolute gold.'*

Matty looked embarrassed and didn't answer, her entire demeanor that of a scolded child. It was like Doctor Wegner was utilizing some sort of Jedi mind trick.

Brenner broke the spell by simply leaning forward and slapping the diminutive elocutionist across the face, snapping his head to one side with the force of the blow. 'Shut it, Rumpelstiltskin,' he said. 'Personally we don't give a shit how disappointed you are. Now, I am going to ask you a few questions, you are going to answer truthfully or things will go badly for you. In all fairness and keeping to the truth in advertising rules, things might go pretty badly for you anyway, but that all remains to be seen. You understand?'

Doctor Wegner nodded and Brenner noted there was no hint of fear or trepidation in the little man's expression. His only look was curiosity and, perhaps, a little disdain.

'We have proof you have been involved with illegal organ harvesting,' said Brenner.

Wegner didn't react for a few seconds, then he raised an eyebrow. 'Sorry,' he said. 'Did you expect a response? It's just that wasn't a question, as such. It was a statement.'

'Do you want me to smack you again?' asked Brenner.

Wegner shook his head. 'No. Why would I?'

'Well, then talk.'

'Oh, I see,' said Wegner. 'It was a declarative question. What you are asking is, am I involved with illegal organ harvesting. Well, the answer to that is almost certainly, yes.'

'Just like that,' said Brenner in disbelief. 'You admit it. No remorse, no guilt.'

'What would be the point in denying it?' asked Wegner. 'Obviously you know, or you wouldn't be here. As to remorse and guilt, just because something is illegal doesn't mean it is morally corrupt or evil. Personally, I know I am doing good. I help people to live. I save lives. Hundreds of lives, how many people can say that?'

Brenner had to marshal his thoughts as the doctor's golden voice washed over him like a balm, soothing his righteous anger and nullifying his thoughts of retribution. After all, he was correct. He was saving lives, albeit with collateral damage. But it was the few being sacrificed for the many.

'You murder innocent people,' said Brenner. 'There's no argument to justify what you are doing. I mean, for fucks sake, it's not like you do it for free. You are making an absolute fortune out of it. According to Griff there are millions involved.'

Wegner nodded. 'Many millions. Hundreds of millions, actually.'

'Well all that money doesn't channel through here,'

observed Brenner. 'So, Wegner, you are going to tell me exactly who else is involved. I want the nuts and bolts of the whole operation, and smartly or I am going to initiate a bit of physical encouragement. Perhaps in the form of broken bones.'

Wegner thought for a few seconds, his head cocked to one side like a particularly odd looking flightless bird. 'No,' he said. 'I don't believe it would be in the organizations best interest to divulge any information.'

Brenner did a double take. 'Are you stupid or something?' he asked. 'Because if you don't believe I'll hurt you, then you are very much mistaken.'

'Oh, I am sure you will carry out your threat,' said Wegner. 'After all, you look like a man of action, a man who would keep their word. I simply do not think spilling the beans would be to my advantage in the slightest.'

Before Brenner could say anything, Matty pulled him to one side. 'Perhaps I should have mentioned before,' she said. 'Wegner has Urbach-Wiethe disease.'

Brenner shook his head. 'Let's assume I have no idea what that is. Because I don't. Explain.'

'It's an extremely rare genetic condition that causes calcium deposits in the brain, although it doesn't affect the persons IQ. Almost every sufferer is affected in a different way. In Wegner's case the disease has caused a hardening of his amygdale.'

'Still not with you,' admitted Brenner.

'He can't feel any fear,' said Matty. 'Other emotions, yes,

but not fear. Not at all.'

'Yeah, definitely something you could have mentioned before,' agreed Brenner. 'However, fear is not always a motivator. But pain is.'

'You can try,' said Matty. 'But even if you break a finger, or something, he will experience the pain but you can't threaten him with it. He will simply not react in a normal way, you see, fear is what helps the human mind to connect certain actions and consequences. Without it, you breaking his finger will simply seem to him like a random act of violence.'

'Let's see,' said Brenner as he leaned over, grabbed Wegner's right-hand ring finger and snapped it.

Wegner squealed in pain.

'So,' said Brenner. 'Are you going to tell me about the operation?'

Wegner shook his head. 'I believe I have already said I won't be doing that.'

'I'll break another finger,' threatened Brenner.

Wegner nodded. 'Yes,' he said. 'I am sure, if you say so, then you will.'

You could avoid it by talking,' explained Brenner.

'I'm sorry but I don't get the connection,' said Wegner, a puzzled look on his face.

Brenner thought for a while, going over the concepts of pain and interrogation in his mind. 'It's a punishment,' he said, eventually. 'I want you to tell me about the operation. If you don't tell me then I will punish you by breaking a finger. Or an arm. Or leg.'

'When will you stop?' asked Wegner. 'Presumably after all my limbs are broken you can no longer punish me. What then.'

'Well then, it's game over,' said Brenner. 'I will admit defeat and I shall kill you. Probably by breaking your neck.'

Wegner frowned. 'That is unacceptable. I would dearly love to avoid dying, so I shall tell you whatever you want to know, with the rider that you will not kill me.'

Brenner nodded. 'I will not kill you, if you are honest with me and hold nothing back.'

'I believe you,' said the doctor. 'What would you like to know?'

19

'Where do the organs go from here?' asked Brenner.

'You have to bear in mind that they have a limited shelf life,' answered Wegner. 'An optimum time period after which they fast become unusable. Lungs, heart, only four to six hours. Even with modern transport there is a limit to how far you can transport something in that time frame. Liver, pancreas, twenty-four hours. Kidneys, much better, around three days. That opens the market up, you can get right across the world in twenty-four hours. Other parts like bone, skin and corneas have a shelf live measured in years, so we tend to have a large stock of those.'

'Look, Frankenstein,' snapped Brenner. 'I'm not interested in the lecture. Where do they go?'

'Mainly to a facility in Houston,' said Wegner. 'A small private hospital registered under the "Meta Global Medical Group". It's situated near the Texas Medical Center. The center has over fifty hospitals and does more than fourteen thousand heart operations a year, and thousands of other organ replacements.'

'Who is in charge there?'

Wegner shook his head. 'I really don't know. I have a list of phone numbers, names, and such. It's in my desk, I think. May I?' He made as if to stand.

Brenner nodded and the doctor walked over to his desk, opened the top drawer, and rummaged through. He obviously didn't find what he wanted and proceeded to the second drawer where he pulled out a small address book. He handed it to Brenner and sat again.

'The relevant numbers are all on the back page. There's only a few and I seldom talk to any of them. Most communication is done via the Dark Web and scrubbed straight afterward. The address to the center is there as well. Now, I believe I have upheld my part of the bargain. I would say it is time you left.'

Matty turned to Brenner and held up her hand. 'Hold on,' she said. 'I might be paranoid but something is wrong.' She stared at Wegner for a few seconds then she spoke. 'Why did you look for the address book in the first drawer when it was in the second drawer?'

Wegner shrugged. 'Forgot where it was.'

Matty shook her head. 'Bullshit. You have an eidetic memory. Perfect recall. You're well-known for that.' She strode over to the desk, pulled open the top drawer and looked inside. Then she ran her finger along the underside of the desk inside the drawer. 'Shit,' she exclaimed. 'It's a panic button. He's called the guards.'

Brenner turned to face Wegner. 'How long?' he asked.

'Surprised that they aren't here already,' replied the doctor. 'So, Mister Brenner,' he continued. 'Looks like the jigs up. Go quietly and you will be treated with compassion.'

'Fuck you,' snapped Brenner. 'What you mean is, go quietly and you will harvest my organs and sell them to the highest bidder.'

Wegner shrugged. 'There will be no pain,' he said. 'We are not barbarians, Mister Brenner. Whatever you may think. We are medical professionals. And think, your sacrifice will result in the prolonging of maybe another six lives. Perhaps even more.'

Before Brenner could answered there was a loud knocking on the door and a guard called out. 'Doctor Wegner. Are you alright?'

Brenner loomed threateningly over the diminutive doctor who said nothing.

The guard banged the door again. 'Doctor, if you don't answer we shall override the locks and come in.'

Brenner started to undress, taking his boots off first then folding his shirt and trousers and laying them on top. Matty picked them up and held them for him.

Wegner gave a double take. 'What the hell are you doing?' he asked. 'Trust me, they'll have the door open long before you can get up to any funny stuff.'

Brenner changed, his body rippling into its Wolfman form in under two seconds.

Wegner's mouth hung open. 'That's impossible,' he mumbled.

'Yet here I am,' pointed out Brenner.

'You're a werewolf,' observed Wegner.

'No,' corrected Brenner. 'I am the result of a United States Army experiment from the nineteen sixties.'

Wegner shook his head and laughed. 'Bullshit,' he stated. 'I have a doctorate in advanced genetics. There is no way anyone could create that sort of transformation. It's simply not possible.'

Brenner shook his head. 'Obviously you're wrong.'

The door started to open before Wegner could espouse any more of his theory. Brenner leaned forward and grabbed the little Frankensteinian doctor by his right ankle and picked him up, dangling him like rag doll.

'We have a deal,' squealed Wegner. 'You said you wouldn't kill me.'

'I just reneged on the deal,' said Brenner. 'Just like you did when you called the guards.'

'What are you going to do with me?' asked Wegner as he dangled in front of Brenner, hanging there by his right foot.

'I'm going to use you as a flail to beat the guards to death,' growled Brenner.

Oh,' exclaimed Wegner, his voice still eerily devoid of fear. 'I see. Irony.'

The door burst open and two guards ran in. Brenner swung Wegner like he was a medieval battle mace, smashing him into the two guards with enough force to splinter bones, smash skulls, and end lives.

He dropped Wegner's corpse to the floor on top of the two dispatched guards and beckoned to Matty.

'Come on, let's get going.'

Matty stood rooted to the spot, appalled at the massive amount of casual violence that had just taken place in front of her. The almost careless way in which Brenner had unceremoniously dispatched three human beings. And the manner in which he had done so. Beating two to death with the third one. Every part of her being told her to run. To run away and hide from the monster.

Then she remembered what Wegner had just admitted to having done. And she recalled he had said she and Brenner would be the next victims in his charnel house production line.

She followed the Wolfman out of the apartment.

'What now?' asked Matty.

'Time for stealth is over,' said Brenner.

'Oh,' reacted Matty. 'So smashing doors down and beating people with other people, that was stealth?'

'Yep,' agreed Brenner. 'Now we got the info we need we get the hell out of here. Griff will cover us and I'll take care of any of the guards he can't sort out.' Brenner stopped walking and swore. 'Shit.'

'What?'

'Griff. I gave all the money away at the last place. Now he doesn't have a place to live. Do you reckon Wegner had any cash in his place?'

'How the hell should I know?' responded Matty. 'Probably. Anything as illegal as he was dealing in always seems to attract a lot of cash. Easier to hide than if you had it in a bank account.'

'My thoughts exactly,' agreed Brenner. 'Let's try to find his stash. We'll give ourselves a minute. No longer. Then we split.'

Matty followed the Wolfman back into the apartment and

they began searching. Checking behind pictures, in desks and cupboards.

While Matty was making an attempt to be methodical, Brenner simply tore things apart, throwing sofas and chairs over his shoulder as he went through the room. Eventually he threw the refrigerator to one side and exposed a wall safe. It was an old fashioned single lock affair with a large steel handle. Brenner broke in to it by simply grabbing the handle and turning until it popped and the door swung open.

'Jackpot,' he growled.

Matty grabbed a rucksack from Wegner's closet and Brenner loaded it with the cash as well as a couple of watches and a diamond pinkie ring.

They left the room again, walking fast and heading for the exit. When they got to the front steel door, Brenner tested to see it was locked and, when he found it was, he put his hand on Matty's chest. 'Stand back,' he growled then unleashed a straight right hand.

The door exploded out, whipping through the air like a giant Frisbee. The two of them ran out of the building, moving right as soon as they were out of the doorway.

'Stay close to me,' instructed Brenner.

Two guards came sprinting around the corner and ran straight into the Wolfman. There was a brief scuffle and a terrible grating sound as bone crushed against bone. Brenner stepped over the two lifeless bodies and Matty followed, trying hard not to look down as she did so.

They heard the sound of running feet as more guards approached but then there was the dull sound of hypersonic lead striking flesh and the running came to an abrupt stop.

The Wolfman smiled. 'Griff,' he said. 'Let's keep going. Head for the main gate.'

Brenner led them around the corner making sure Matty was protected by his bulk, putting his body between her and any prospective danger. Shots rang out and puffs of sand flew up as the rounds struck the ground near them.

Griff's rifle spat lead and a guard went down.

But there were more to take his place.

The Wolfman, hurdled a wooden barrier and grabbed the two guards behind it, crushing their necks, one in each massive hand. Then he gestured for Matty to follow. They had almost made it to the gate when a guard on one of the towers opened up on them with an automatic weapon. The spiteful crack and buzz of bullets whipped the air around them, plucking with fingers of hot lead, seeking to kill and maim.

Brenner pulled Matty back behind the corner of the building, taking cover from the fire. He peeked around the corner to see Griff was trying to get a bead on the guard in the tower but the angle was all wrong and the tower was well protected with steel plate and sandbags.

Brenner made a decision. 'Wait,' he growled at Matty as he took off at speed, running toward the tower. Bullets churned up the soil around him as he ran, jinking from side to side to spoil the gunman's aim. But the shooter was good and, before he was halfway there, a round struck Brenner in his chest, spinning him around on his feet.

But the Wolfman regained his balance and continued running, his speed unabated. At the last moment, Brenner dropped his shoulder and thundered into one of the four steel supports holding up the guard tower. There was a massive boom as he struck home and the pinion buckled and broke. The tower shivered for a few seconds then slowly collapsed to the ground, throwing the hapless guard clear as it did. In two bounds, the Wolfman was on him. A second later he was no longer a threat.

Brenner stood still for a while, shaking his head. Even for the Wolfman, he had taken some serious hits. A gunshot wound, then a head on collision with a nigh immovable object had taken its toll and he needed a few seconds to reset.

Griff's rifle cracked again and the final two guards fell to the floor.

Matty ran up to Brenner and grabbed his arm. 'Come on, big boy,' she said. 'Let's get moving before any reinforcements arrive.'

Brenner allowed himself to be led, through the gates and toward Griff's position.

Beauty and the beast.

When they reached Griff, Brenner's compos was fully mentis again.

'Thanks, Griff,' he said. 'Good shooting.'

'Cool,' replied Griff. 'Let's get the hell out of Dodge. I

assume you've taken care of business?'

'And how,' agreed Brenner. 'Kicked ass and took names. Also got this,' he held out the rucksack full of cash.

Griff opened it and peeked inside. 'Oh yes,' he exclaimed. 'Mama's gonna buy a brand-new pair of shoes. Let's move.'

The three of them took off, jogging slowly toward the hidden Range Rover.

20

Griff drove. They were heading back to chief Kohana's dwellings but Brenner asked his friend to take a detour to one of the farms. The one The Pastor had lived at. He wanted to show Matty part of what they were fighting for.

When they pulled up outside the main house, Antonio Martinez was already waiting for them. 'Greetings,' he called, as they got out of the Range Rover.

Both Brenner and Griff shook his hand then Brenner introduced Matty.

'Antonio,' he said. 'This is my friend, Doctor Materia Santiago. Materia, this is Antonio Martinez, the leader of this budding commune.'

Matty held out her hand. 'Call me Matty,' she said.

Antonio nodded but said nothing, his demeanor quiet and taciturn. Not a man given to trivialities or small talk.

Antonio gave them all a quick tour, showing them his plans for the farm, introducing people by name and generally proving Brenner had made the correct choice by putting him in charge.

'Anything else you need?' asked Brenner.

Antonio shook his head. 'We are fine. Some people have decided to leave. To return to the lives they once had. Most, however, are staying. We plan for the future but we have decided not to dictate how long that future will extend to. In a way, I suppose, we are simply living in the moment.'

'A lot to be recommended about that,' said Brenner. 'No problem with the sheriff? Any other unwanted visitors?'

'We did have some visitors,' admitted Antonio. 'They were strange. Harmless, but strange.'

'Don't tell me,' said Brenner. 'Two old men, worn clothes, brought their own moonshine, drank, didn't hardly speak. Next thing they were gone.'

Antonio raised an eyebrow. The closest Brenner had ever seen him to being surprised. 'Exactly. Friends of yours?'

'No. Acquaintances, I suppose. Did they say anything at all?'

'One thing,' admitted Antonio. 'But it made no sense. The one said to me, this is important, now. That's all. Then when I looked for them again, they were gone.'

Brenner shook his head, exasperated. 'Don't worry about it. You're doing well. So, cool. Be safe. We're off.'

The three of them left. Matty waved goodbye. Antonio did not. He wasn't being unfriendly, he was simply, being. Greetings and goodbyes were unnecessary societal norms his recent experiences had cauterized from his system.

Soon they were pulling up outside chief Kohana's loose cluster of dwellings. As was his usual custom, Kohana was seated under his makeshift awning, smoking his pipe.

Opposite him where two old men.

Mister Reeve and Mister Bolin. Their ever-present bottle of clear liquor stood on the table between them.

Brenner and Griff approached with Matty bringing up the rear.

'Gentlemen,' greeted Brenner.

Kohana stood and shook his hand. The two misters toasted him without talking.

Then Matty stepped forward and both Mister Reeve and Mister Bolin did a double take.

'My goodness me,' said Mister Bolin. 'Now that is an unusual sight. How long would you say since we saw the last one, Mister Reeve?'

'Oh, I reckon at least a few decades.'

'What are you two reprobates talking about?' asked Brenner.

'Why, we are discussing the healer, of course,' answered Mister Reeve.

'You know I'm a doctor?' asked Matty. 'How?'

Mister Reeve raised an eyebrow. 'A doctor as well. That should prove helpful with the healing. Never turn down a decent bit of education I always say.'

Matty shook her head. 'You guys are weird.'

Brenner chuckled. 'You have no idea,' he said. 'Anyway, Mister Reeve, Mister Bolin, this is Doctor Materia Santiago. Matty these are the Watchers. Don't ask, just accept. Mister Reeve and Mister Bolin.'

'Is it true?' asked Kohana, as he stared at Matty, his eyes pools of respect. 'Are you really a healer? I mean, I have heard stories. The elders sometimes spoke of them, but never have I met one.'

Matty looked suitably baffled. 'Look, I studied medicine, but I specialize in research now. I'm sure I can still heal but

I must admit to being a bit rusty.'

Mister Reeve laughed. 'She doesn't know,' he said.

'I have a young man here,' continued Kohana. 'He fell off his motorbike yesterday. Broke his leg rather badly. We have done what we can but I would be grateful if you, a healer, could take a look at him.'

'Of course,' said Matty. 'But without x-rays or a medical kit I am not sure what I can do.'

'Come,' Kohana said as he walked away.

The entire group, including the Watchers, followed the chief to a large tent. Kohana went inside and the rest trooped in behind him.

Lying on a low bed was a young man, he was covered with a light cotton sheet, his face wet with sweat, asleep but tossing and turning. Feverish. His right leg stuck out from the sheet. Two wooden splints and bandages.

Matty knelt next to him, took his pulse, and laid her hand on his forehead to check his temperature.

Then she stripped off the bandage and the splints. The leg was swollen and discolored.

'It's infected,' she said. 'The bone has splintered. I am afraid there is nothing I can do. He needs a surgery. Hospital, or he will lose the leg. Most probably his life as well. I am so sorry.'

'Heal him,' said Mister Bolin, his voice low and serious. Not commanding nor insisting. Merely a statement.

'How, you crazy old man?' snapped Matty. 'I've already told you what I need to help him. Shit,' she cursed.

The young man mumbled and cried out in his delirium the pain overcoming his stupor. Matty leaned forward and held his leg, running her hands along the wound in an unconscious effort to smooth away the pain. To help in some way. But as her hands touched his leg, she gasped and her eyes rolled back in their sockets exposing the whites. Then she started to shiver like a hypothermia victim and her breath came in short ragged gasps.

Her hands clamped down on the man's swollen flesh and he cried out in pain from the pressure, but Matty didn't pull back. In fact, she squeezed harder, panting at the same time, her chest rising and falling in swift sharp movements.

Brenner stepped forward. 'What the hell?'

But Kohana stopped him. 'No, wait,' he said. 'I have heard stories of this from the tribal elders. Leave her, she is in no danger. Nor is Simon.'

Matty shook for another twenty seconds or so then her body went limp, her eyes closed and her death-grip relaxed, allowing her hands to slide off the young man's damaged leg. Within moments she opened her eyes and was back to normal. Breathing slow and steady, no shaking.

They all leaned forward and looked at the leg. The swelling had gone down and much of the discoloration had disappeared.

Matty smiled. 'I did that,' she said to Brenner, her voice filled with both pride and disbelief. 'It was like I could see right into his flesh. Become part of it. I burned out the poisons, pushed the bone together, encouraged the flesh to heal. I did it.'

'Well done,' said Mister Reeve. 'You are a healer.'

'I don't get it,' says Griff. 'So, she just laid hands on the boy and healed him?'

Matty shook her head. 'Not quite. The bone is still broken, and he has much recovery to do. But I helped. I sped up the process. I healed him enough to take him out of danger.'

'That is how it works,' said Mister Bolin 'But remember, sometimes a person is too far gone. Other times they will simply not respond. We have also found that the more "civilized" a person the less a healer can help. Modernity, obsession with technology, it all has its price.'

Kohana turned to face Matty and bowed deeply. 'My thanks, healer,' he said. 'Now please, let us return to my abode, there we shall eat and drink.'

Most of the tribe collected around the table and the news of the healer was the buzz of the meal.

Matty didn't say much but, after they had eaten, she leaned into Brenner and spoke directly to him.

'I have thought about it and I have decided to stay on here as a doctor, a healer. Not only here but also at the farms. I will speak to Antonio and ask if we can turn the main house into some sort of clinic. Mini-hospital. At least for a while. Until I get my head around this whole, "Healer" thing.'

Brenner agreed. He took the rucksack and placed it on the table. He started to take money out and count it into piles.

Griff looked over and sighed. 'Damn it. Brenner is giving away my money again. He's determined this old man here should stay homeless until he dies. No Winnebago, no computers, no way to make a living. It's cruel, that's what it is.'

'Hey, calm down, old man,' said Brenner.

'Hey, you're actually six months older than me,' argued Griff. 'So quit the ageist slurs. Douchebag.'

'Whatever,' countered Brenner as he pushed a stack of money across the table to Matty. 'This should be enough to set up a medical center and whatever else you need. Use it wisely.' Then he pushed the rucksack over to Griff. 'And this is for the homeless dude,' he grinned. 'Should be enough there to get a new set up.'

Griff took a quick look and laughed. 'Man, this is enough to get a new Cummins diesel Grand Tour series Winnebago with every luxury known to man, and some that aren't known yet. Also a full range of computer upgrades and specialized armor and a weapons suite. Cool. Exceptionally cool.' He stood, took out his cell phone, dialed and started talking, walking away as he did, gesticulating and shouting. The only words Brenner could pick up were, "cash" and "shut up and listen".

'So, what next?' asked chief Kohana.

'Off to Houston,' replied Brenner. 'Places to go, people to kill. You know how it is.'

Kohana chuckled.

'Dallas,' interrupted Griff who had just gotten off his cell phone.

'What?' asked Brenner.

'We gotta go to Dallas first. Pick up my new rig. Then onto Houston.'

'We can sort that all out after Houston,' said Brenner. 'We'll take the bike. The sooner we get this done the better.'

'No way,' argued Griff. 'Trust me on this, Ded. It'll be worth the few days wait.'

'Few days?'

'Yeah. And another thing,' continued Griff. 'There is no way on God's green earth that I'm riding pillion with you on that rat bike. Contrary to what you may think, I do not have a death wish. I'll drive the Range Rover and you can follow on that deathtrap of yours.'

Brenner didn't bother dissenting. It was obvious his friend's mind was set, and he knew better than to argue with him. 'Fine, let's say our goodbyes and be on our way.'

There was a general shaking of hands and a patting of backs. No one was surprised to find the Watchers were no longer there. Obviously, goodbyes were not important enough to watch.

Before they left, Brenner took Matty to one side. 'This healing thing,' he said. 'Could it work on me?'

'You're hurt?' asked Matty.

Brenner nodded. 'The curse. Could you take it away? Could you encourage my body to start to heal?'

'I don't think it works like that,' said Matty.

'But you don't know,' urged Brenner. 'It might. Please.'

Matty nodded. 'Okay. I'll take a look,' she agreed. Then she laid her hands on his chest and closed her eyes. After a few seconds she started to shake, then she flew backward like someone had attached a rope to her and given it a yank. She hit the ground over twenty feet away, screaming and shivering, her breath a steam train, her heart hammering like a small animal trapped in a cage.

Brenner ran to her, ready to help. But she held her hands up. 'No,' she yelled. 'Get back. Don't touch me. Please.'

The big man turned and walked away, an indescribable expression of pain on his face.

'I'm sorry,' whispered Matty.

Griff rushed over and helped the healer to her feet. 'I saw that,' he said. 'What the hell. What happened? What did you see? Are you hurt?'

'I'm alright,' said Matty. 'But as to what I saw, I don't think I can put it into words,'

'Try,' insisted Griff. 'What scared you so much?'

'It's Brenner, he is more than what he is.' Matty waved her hands in front of her face, grasping for words. 'He is more than a man. More than a wolf.'

'Duh,' said Griff. 'He is a Wolfman.'

Matty shook her head. 'On the surface. But he is much more than that.' She took a shaky breath. 'My god, the pain.'

'He hurt you?'

'No, *his* pain. I felt it. That poor man. His life is a constant battle against the wolf. How he keeps it in check is beyond me. His strength of character is unbelievable. His soul is like a caged animal, constantly banging against the bars in an effort to escape, to maim, to kill everything it sees. But Brenner keeps it at bay. Somehow, he does. But there is more. For a fleeting second, I saw deeper. It was Brenner, but it wasn't.'

'What do you mean?'

Matty shook her head. 'In my mind's eye, I saw him in a true light and, just for the briefest second he seemed shrouded in shadow, as if a cloak of darkness had been draped over him. And then he turned and looked at me and I saw them. It wasn't a cloak of shadow. It was obvious what they were.'

'What?'

'His wings. Huge and dark and powerful. I saw Brenner's wings. I saw the wings of a dark angel.' Matty started to cry. 'Protect him, Griff. Help him. He is so desperately alone.'

'I'll try, my girl,' said Griff, his voice rough with emotion. 'I'll try.'

21

Griff had a satnav in the Range Rover so he led and Brenner followed. They drove below the speed limit. Steady. Brenner lost himself in the road. He let his mind become the endless black ribbon of blacktop stretching before them.

Never starting, never ending. An asphalt artery in the body of the country he loved. A country he had fought for.

A country that had betrayed him.

But, try as he might to empty his mind, he couldn't dispel the look of fear he had seen on Matty's face. Or her words. *"Don't touch me"*.

He could see Griff was on his cell phone. Obviously talking to the vehicle dealer they were on their way to see.

Three more hours into the nine-hour trip, Griff slowed down and started to pull over. Brenner saw where he was heading. A large shack, seemingly built in the middle of nowhere. Outside stood a few eighteen wheelers and a row of bikes. Smoke wafted from a set of chimneys and Brenner's enhanced sense of smell meant he didn't have need of the hand-painted sign that read— *'Bubba's BBQ. The best in the west'*.

The two of them parked up and Griff led the way. The one side of the shack was open to the elements. A row of BBQ's lined the far wall. Tending them, a massive redneck, blue dungarees, no shirt, beat up Stetson, and a neckerchief the size of a bed sheet.

Griff threw down a pile of cash. 'Beer. Ice cold. Six-pack.' Then he pointed at Brenner. 'And feed him. Meat. Beef. Rare. As much as he wants.'

The redneck nodded without speaking and took the cash. Seconds later a six-pack of Bud was laid on the table. Griff opened one and slid it to Brenner who downed it without taking it from his lips. Griff passed another one over.

As Brenner started on that one, the redneck slammed a huge wooden platter onto the tabletop. It was laden with steak. Rump. Bleeding. At least six pounds of it. No sides. No fork. Simply two large, sharp knives.

Brenner set to.

Half an hour later the redneck placed another platter on the table with another six-pack. He nodded his approval and left.

Finally, Brenner leaned back in his chair, replete. He extracted two cigarettes, lit them, and handed one to Griff. The patrons of Bubba's BBQ paid scant attention to the no smoking laws.

'You wanna talk?' asked Griff.

'I scared her.'

Griff nodded. 'Yes. You did. But you didn't mean to. And anyway, she was scared for you, not of you.'

Brenner shrugged. 'Potato–patahtoh. You know, I thought we might have had something. There was a connection. But now she's a healer, whatever that is, and I'm … well … what's the opposite of a healer?'

'A killer.'

Brenner flinched.

'Sorry,' apologized Griff.

'No need to be sorry,' admitted Brenner. 'You're one hundred percent correct. Talk about diametrically opposed. You two had a long chat. What else did she say?'

'Nothing much,' said Griff, not wanting to trouble his friend any further. 'Just girl shit. You finished? We should truck on.'

Brenner nodded, and they left.

22

They arrived at Dallas in the early evening and Brenner followed Griff through a series of semi-deserted roads deep into the industrial section on the outskirts of the city.

Although Dallas is a thriving city with nine Forbes 500 companies and a massive tech industry, there are always areas to be found where the less wholesome gather.

The darker underbelly of the city. Boarded up shops, broken lights, graffiti, and a seeming preponderance of shadow.

The places where men like Griff and Brenner thrived.

The jungle.

Griff pulled up outside a light industrial warehouse. Lights were on inside and access was restricted by a chain-link fence and a high, electrically powered steel gate. Griff took out his cell and made a call. A couple of minutes later there was a grinding of gears and the gate slid to one side.

The two men drove in and the gate closed behind them.

A man walked over to greet them.

Short, wiry, unshaven. Teeth that could snack on an apple through a tennis racket. Grease-stained denims, a string vest, and steel-capped work boots.

He shook Griff by the hand.

'Weasel, Brenner. Brenner, Weasel,' Griff grunted the introductions. 'He's a complete dick, but a genius when it comes to personalizing recreational vehicles to the degree I demand.'

Weasel's expression showed a brief flash of irritation at Griff's comment but he didn't say anything, instead merely beckoning for them to follow him.

They followed the dude into the workshop.

There stood a huge Winnebago. Shining like a mythical beast. All around it unopened boxes of computer parts, thick sheets of polycarbonate bullet proof material. Carbon fiber, Kevlar sheets, satellite components. Smoke grenades. Even what looked like a rotary-fed shotgun.

'Man, what the hell is going down here?' asked Brenner. 'Looks like we're preparing for a massive showdown. Freaking Cambodia, man.'

'Upgrades,' said Griff. 'No one is going to catch the old man with his pants down again. Look, Weasel, I need this shit going in three days.'

The skinny man sucked air through his teeth, like Griff had just demanded he find the Holy Grail. 'No can do, Griff,' he said. 'The mere fact I got this stuff here is a minor miracle. You just gonna have to bite down and wait.' As he spoke two more men slid out of the shadows and stood beside him. They were of the same type. Hard and spare. Men accustomed to casual violence.

'Hey, we had a deal,' said Griff. 'Bear in mind I haven't paid yet.'

'Well, you know what they say ... deals are made to be broken. As for withholding payment, look Griff, you got nowhere else to go. I'm doing you a favor. Chill, come back in a few days and we'll talk delivery times. Oh, and now you've brought the cash up,' he held his hand out. 'I'd appreciate a big wad of paper right about now.'

Griff shook his head in disgust. 'Weasel, you really are an utter shit,' he said. 'Also, stupid. Now being a shithead is fine by me, but stupid wins no prizes.' He turned to Brenner. 'Hey, Ded. Talk nicely to Mister Weasel here, it seems like he needs a bit of motivation.'

Brenner walked over. He moved slowly, like a human landscape. A mountain. Or a glacier. Something natural and unstoppable. The tension in the air was palpable. The two newcomers stood straighter. Readying themselves

Weasel grinned, confident in his assumed superior bargaining position. 'Hey, big man,' he said. 'Hope you ain't trying to intimidate the Weasel, because I don't sweat you.'

Griff shook his head again. 'As I said, stupid.'

Brenner took a wad of cash from his pocket and held it in front of Weasel's face. 'This is what we call, the carrot.' Then he grabbed Weasel by the throat, his huge hands encircling the wiry man's neck completely. He started to squeeze, eliciting a muted squeak from the rodent-like man.

The two men moved forward to protect their boss. Brenner didn't even bother to pocket the money he was holding in his hand. Still holding Weasel by the neck, he lashed out, hand moving so fast it was a mere blur. Both men hit the deck like a grand piano had just fallen on them.

Brenner growled softly. 'And this is what we call, the stick.' He shook Weasel again, taking care not to irreparably crush his throat as he did so. 'In three days' time, we will return. I hope to give you the carrot. Do not make me use the stick. Trust me, it could well prove to be a terminal error on your part.'

'Okay, Ded. Cool it. If you kill him, then we're even worse off,' interjected Griff.

Brenner growled once more then dropped Weasel to the floor.

Weasel shook himself like a wet dog, coughed a few times then took a deep breath. 'Sure thing, man. Sure thing. I'll get all my guys onto it. Work twenty-four-hour shifts. Best quality. We'll deliver, man. Enough of the choking and beating on my employees already. Sheesh. I'll deliver.'

Brenner nodded. 'I know. Come on, Griff, let's split.'

The big man followed Griff back toward the center of the city, frowning slightly as his friend headed toward the more salubrious parts of the town.

Finally, he pulled up outside the Ritz Hotel.

Brenner glanced around, taking in the upmarket bars and restaurants, the distinct lack of graffiti and the decidedly obvious dearth of Harley Davidsons.

'Wassup?' he demanded of Griff. 'This is a little outside the usual low-level snake pit we typically frequent.'

'What the hell,' observed the old man. 'We deserve a bit of R&R. Feather pillows, working plumbing, and sheets that don't scratch the crap outa you.'

The valet walked over, and Griff handed him the Range Rover keys.

'You can park the bike there,' the valet told Brenner as he pointed at a small parking area, off to the left of the entrance.

Brenner parked, and they went inside.

Griff asked for a two-bedroom suite and there was a momentary period of confusion when both of the friends realized neither had any form of legal ID. This was quickly solved by Griff laying down a huge wedge of cash on the reception desk. 'Security deposit,' he said.

The bell hop showed them to the suite and Griff tipped him, even though they had no bags to carry save the rucksack full of cash Griff kept a death-grip on.

'We can start to recce tomorrow,' said Brenner, ignoring the surrounding opulence. 'Grab something to chow, bed down, get an early start.'

Griff laughed. 'Man, you are one Calvinistic mother. All work and no play makes Ded a boring SOB. I told you, R&R. Every good soldier needs a break. Fucking Saigon, man. Shit, shower, shave. Drink, gamble, poontang. No recce. We hit the trail again when the Winnebago is up and running. Trust me, we need it. Then I can hack into their computers, get blueprints of buildings, see into their bank accounts. Trust me, Ded, intel is king. R&R, then plan, then we do it.'

Brenner agreed, albeit begrudgingly. He knew once Griff had his teeth into an idea, then it was almost impossible to prize him off. And, to be fair, they had stopped the supply of "organ donors" as well as destroying any chance the chain could be fixed, so it was now merely a case of mopping up. No one would suffer from a couple of days of inaction, and a bit of R&R sounded great, even though it did grate against his usual abstemious principles.

'Right,' said Griff, after they had hit the showers. 'Next, to the men's outfitters downstairs to overpay for some halfway reasonable clothes. You look like a bum. And, to be honest, I'm not far off myself. After that, I feel like a game of poker. I'll speak to the concierge, see if he can't rustle us up a game. Straight five card draw, none of this Texas hold 'em crap. I wanna play real poker.'

'Why the need for poker?' asked Brenner.

Griff shrugged. 'Blast from the past. I like cards, just not very good at them. But if I recall, you can't lose.'

'Yep,' agreed Brenner. 'And that's why I won't be playing.'

'No way,' argued Griff. 'One of the main reasons I wanna do this is so I can lose and you can take up the slack. All the gain with no pain.'

'It's too close to cheating,' said Brenner. 'I can smell their emotions, judge their reactions. They're like prey. They cannot hide from the wolf. The wolf cannot be bluffed.'

'That's not cheating,' stated Griff. 'That's natural selection. The Darwin principle. Culling the weak from the pack.'

Brenner laughed. 'Okay, fine. I'll play. But not high stakes stuff. I'll do nickel and dime. I'm not a cardsharp. And besides, whenever I find myself in a high-stakes game, things always go to shit in a handbag. I don't know what it is, but I just seem to attract trouble like dog shit attracts flies.'

Griff shook his head. 'Not true, Ded. You don't attract trouble as such. You uncover wrongdoings. Or more specifically, people who do wrong. If there is an asshole out there, you will expose them. Basically, you're an asshole magnet.'

Brenner chuckled. 'Thanks. Not sure if that's better or worse.'

'Both,' said Griff. 'Come on, let's get kitted out.'

'I'm not wearing a suit,' warned Brenner.

'No, of course not. Just some chinos, shirt, good leather jacket. You can keep the work boots.'

'Man, Griff, money sure burns a hole in your pocket.'

'It's only paper. Easy come, easy go.'

They went downstairs and Griff got kitted first. Then while the assistant was setting up Brenner, the old man conversed with the concierge, explaining his need for a friendly poker match.

Brenner walked out and Griff held a thumb up. Both of the men were dressed in nondescript smart casual. The clothes were expensive, well-fitting and in various shades of khaki, olive, and brown. Urban camo.

The concierge had already organized a driver and, minutes later, the two friends were on their way to the game. Neither had any idea where they were going but it was obvious from the surrounds they were heading for an upmarket residential area.

They arrived and entered the property via an open iron gate and a long driveway. At the door, they were met by two goons in cheap suits and shown to the playing area. The game hadn't started yet. Four men sat at the baize-covered table. One man stood and greeted them.

'Evening, gentlemen,' he said. 'Jimmy from the Ritz has vouched for you so that's all good. My name is Andy. These three gentlemen are Cooper, Angus, and Simon. Regulars at the game so it's nice to get some new blood, as it were.'

Griff introduced both himself and Brenner and they sat down after ordering beer from one of the goons.

'Right,' said Andy. 'As I'm sure you know, five card draw, rotating deal, five-hundred-dollar ante.'

Brenner scowled and whispered to Griff, *sotto voce*. 'This isn't nickel and dime, dude, this is serious game.'

Griff grinned. 'Yeah, sorry about that. Only game the concierge could find at such short notice.'

The beers were brought, and the game commenced.

Griff played poker like a man charging a machine gun nest. Head down, no bluffing, and balls to the wall. If he won a hand, it was pure luck. Mainly, he lost.

Brenner, however, was the diametric opposite. He played cards like he was on deep recon. Every movement a lesson in subtlety. Every decision taken as a life or death choice. Building a catalog of the other players' tells, foibles, and emotional idiosyncrasies. And when he was secure in his knowledge, he struck, winning three big hands in a row, calling a bluff and handing out one of his own.

As the evening wore on, Griff continued to lose, but Brenner didn't begrudge him one dollar. The old man was thoroughly enjoying himself, throwing money at ludicrous bets, consuming bottles of cold beer and dealing like a pro, spinning cards across the table and grinning at every hand.

He was having fun and Brenner was more than making up for the losses, building a large pile of cash in front of him.

The deal rotated and Cooper started to flick the cards out, his movements practiced and precise. At the same time, he kept up a running chatter. Like a sideshow carnie. Head bobbing. Winking, laughing.

Distracting.

And Brenner moved. There was no actual perception of movement from the big man. One moment he was seated, and the very next perceivable instant he was standing over Cooper, his massive hand enveloping the dealer's hands and applying a crushing force.

Cooper let out an involuntary squeak of pain and shock.

'I don't take kindly to cheating,' said Brenner, His voice calm. Flat.

'What? Bullshit,' shouted Cooper. 'This game's clean. Fuck you. Boys,' he shouted to the goons. 'Sort this asshat out.'

Before anyone could move, Brenner squeezed harder and the audible sound of bones breaking sounded across the room. Then he lay Cooper's broken mitts down and said to

Andy. 'Flip the pack over.'

Andy did so.

'Check out the bottom four cards,' continued Brenner.

Andy flipped the bottom four cards over and placed them face up on the table. All four aces.

'Bottom dealing,' stated Brenner. 'You,' he pointed at Angus. 'And Cooper, are working together.'

'You bastards,' said Andy, his face white with rage. 'I trusted you two. How long has this been going on? Whatever,' he turned to the two goons. 'Get them out of here. Keep their cash, wallets, watches, jewelry. Make sure they never get in here again.'

The two bouncers did as they were instructed and booted the two cheaters out.

After that the game ended, the mood broken. The bouncers called a cab for Griff and Brenner who went outside to have a smoke and wait in the fresh air.

'Assholes,' said Griff. 'Cheating like that. How did we make out?'

Brenner shrugged. 'Didn't count. Well enough, I'm sure.' Then, without warning he grabbed Griff and dragged him to the floor, rolling hard and fast as he did so. The air above them was buffeted with a passing shot, the sound muted. A silenced weapon.

Griff and Brenner ran behind a car for cover.

'What the hell?' shouted Griff.

'It's that asshole magnet thing,' answered Brenner. 'Seems like our erstwhile gambling companions didn't take kindly to being called out as cheats. They want some payback. I must admit, didn't think they were that pissed at us.'

'Well I'm getting too old for this shit,' said Griff. 'And anyway, I'm on R&R. Can't you sort this out? Without going Wolfman, I mean. Kinda try to be subtle.'

'Oh, subtle,' quipped Brenner. 'Yeah, I remember that. Not sure if I can do it.'

He moved fast and invisible. Becoming the dark.

The horrific sound of solid meaty hits thudded through the night air. Cooper flew through the air, spinning like a top and landing on a nearby car roof, smashing all the windows and setting the alarm off. He groaned softly then lay still, his chest rising and falling in ragged gasps.

'I said subtle,' shouted Griff.

'This is me being subtle,' said Brenner as he walked out into the open. 'It was just the two of them. The other one is sleeping off his error back there. Bloody weekend warriors. Amateurs. Oh, there's our cab.'

The two of them got in and told the driver to head back to the Ritz.

23

They didn't play any more poker. But the next three days were spent drinking, eating far too much, and sleeping whenever they felt like it. And although Brenner didn't go so far as to actually say it, Griff had been right. The rest and recuperation had done him the power of good.

On the third day, Griff took the Range Rover and Brenner followed him to go and pick up the Winnebago.

Weasel had done an awesome job. But even his pride in his work could not cover the guarded expression of hatred he harbored for Brenner.

Regardless, he took them through the many upgrades and additions to the leisure vehicle. They included bullet resistant polycarbonate windows, Kevlar sheeting in the body panels, run-flat tires, and an old-fashioned oil smoke generator, like a Second World War battle ship, perfect for escaping under cover.

There were also upgraded lights, both spot and flood. A James Bond-type caltrop distributor in the back, toggle a switch and you could dump one thousand tire-defeating steel spikes onto the road to discourage any pursuers.

That was topped off with a full suite of computers with double sat-links, all encrypted, a fully-stocked gun safe, triple-lock doors with fingerprint recognition, and an extended self-seal gas tank. One could safely say Griff's new home had all the necessary toys.

Then Weasel showed them a lift on the back for the Harley and even Brenner had to smile. The big man stowed his bike, handed over the carrot and the two of them climbed into the monstrous vehicle and drove away.

In the rearview mirror, they could both plainly see Weasel giving them the finger, a sneer of hatred on his rodent-like face.

Griff took them out of town, driving and testing the vehicle to its limits. After an hour of pushing hard, he declared himself well pleased.

Then he proceeded to take a few back roads, heading further out into the vast open countryside, finally stopping when they were alone, on a stretch of dirt road that looked as if it came from nowhere and went to the same destination.

Griff grabbed a beer from the well-stocked fridge, went into the computer area, fired up the equipment and got to work.

Brenner decided to check out the gun safe. Two AR15's, a pair of colt 45's, and an M24 Remington sniper rifle. For want of something better to do, he stripped the weapons down, cleaned them, and reassembled them. He took his time, slipping into an almost fugue state as he worked on the steel dealers of death.

The art of Zen firearm cleaning.

After a while, Griff shook his head and leaned back in his chair. His expression showed his concern.

'I fucked-up,' he said.

Brenner didn't say anything. He simply waited.

'You said we should have gotten straight onto the hospital dudes,' continued Griff. 'But I thought some rest and recuperation would behoove us. Big mistake. I've been checking out their organizations comms on the Dark Net … they know we're coming for them. They got descriptions. They've tripled their overwatch. Assigned troops of personal bodyguards to all the participating doctors and money men. Man, I'm sorry, Ded. I fucked-up big time. Getting old, dude. Tired.'

'Any mention of the Wolfman?' asked Brenner.

Griff shook his head. 'Nothing. Not even a mention of the farms. All the comms originated from the research center. Obviously, we didn't take out all the guards. Plus, there must have been more people intimately involved in the scheme. Doctor Frankenstein could not have performed those ops by himself. I should have seen this coming.'

Brenner shrugged. 'Not a problem. Still same old, same old. We find them, we fuck them up, we go. Simple.'

Griff laughed. 'Master strategy, oh wise and powerful Wolfman.'

'Hey,' argued Brenner. 'It works. No reason to overcomplicate things. I accept the fact I'm a battering ram, not a scalpel.'

'Okay, fine. As far as our descriptions go that's pretty easy to change. Tell you what, you cut that long hair of yours to a buzz cut and shave your beard. Maybe add a pair of douchebag round spectacles and no one will recognize you.

I'll stop shaving, maybe dye my hair black, little pencil mustache, green contacts. This will work.'

Brenner shook his head. 'When did you last see me with short hair and fully shaved?' he asked.

Griff thought for a while. 'Don't know. Back in the day?'

Brenner nodded. 'I can't cut my hair or shave. Well, I mean, of course I can, but it grows straight back. Within a couple of hours. Something to do with the whole wolf thing. So, what you see is what you get.'

'Well, fuck them then,' snapped Griff. 'They make us, we take them out.'

'That's what I said,' countered Brenner. 'Battering ram. Plus, they have actually made our job much easier. If you say they have assigned troops of bodyguards to the important dudes, then all we need to do is find out who has extra guards and we know that they are the ones to take out. Nice and simple.'

Griff laughed again. 'Right. Let's make a plan then. I think we'll designate this, Operation Battering Ram.'

Brenner laughed.

24

Johnathan Billoti stood with his arms behind his back and looked out of the window. The view from the twentieth-floor corner office was magnificent. He well remembered his humble beginnings. Working his way up through the family, starting with nickel-and-dime jobs and ending up controlling the entire downtown and surrounds.

Those were the days when he had still been known as *Jonny Sausage*, a nickname given him because his off-the-rack suits were always too tight. He had that sort of a build. Barrel-like body, neck as stout as a bull-mastiff's, legs like oil drums, and arms that were short and thick. So, if he purchased a suit which wasn't ridiculously long in the arms or legs then it was sausage-skin tight on the rest of him.

But now he was known as *Cigar Jonny*, courtesy of the Gurkha Black Dragon cigars he smoked. He was never seen in public without one of the horrendously expensive tubes of hand rolled tobacco clamped firmly in his meaty jaw.

And nowadays his suits were all hand-tailored.

Truth be told, many still called him *Jonny Sausage* behind his back. Because no amount of tailoring could turn that Sasquatch of a body into a thing of either beauty or sophistication. As is often said, you simply cannot polish a turd. But Jonny had done the best he could with a bad hand.

Besides his tailored suits, he had explored many other

avenues in his quest to become a man of sophistication. Opera, cocktail parties, black-tie events, and charity balls all featured highly on Jonny's "things-to-do" list. He had even purchased works of art that had been recommended to him. Not stuff he considered to be art. Not paintings of landscapes, or the sea. Or even portraits. No, he had purchased meaningless squiggles. Modern art. Primary-colored pieces of crap he didn't even know which way to hang. But he knew it was the correct thing to do. The societally accepted thing for a man of his wealth to buy.

He was desperate to be thought of as a cerebral businessman, as opposed to a scary thug who thought physical intimidation was a valid negotiating tool and a baseball bat was standard boardroom equipment.

He turned from the window to address the other man in the room. This man was Jonny's opposite in many ways. Slim to the point of malnourished. An off-the-rack suit that fitted like designer apparel. And where Jonny Cigar's eyes and demeanor spoke of passion and appetite and desire, this man's eyes spoke of no such emotions.

They were like two shiny black pebbles, their moisture the only sign they were living material. They were the eyes of a predator. A Komodo dragon. Deep and dark, unblinking. Calculating.

At first glance, one would have been excused for thinking he was the family hit man. The wet work specialist with cold eyes, colder heart, and a steady aim.

In fact, he was far more dangerous than that. He was the

family accountant. He was Jonny's bean counter. Nowadays people tend to think bean counters are simply nitpicking accountant types arguing over the cost of trivialities. This is not true. A real bean counter is a cost and risk analysis specialist. He will look at a situation and decide whether to spend money on it, or simply let it take its course and settle up when all is done.

This is famously called the Ford Pinto effect, named after the Ford company who, when discovering their new compact vehicle was prone to catastrophic failure in a collision which would result in the gas tank rupturing, the bean counters worked out that only one hundred eighty people would burn to death as a result. They deduced that paying their bereaved families off would be cheaper than fixing the problem.

And that is why a bean counter can be deadlier than a hitman. There are few killers who have put one hundred eighty people into the earth.

Very few.

'So, lay it out for me, Harry,' said Cigar Jonny. 'Cut through the crap and tell me what's really going on.'

'Difficult one, Mister C. The doctors have gone apeshit; emailing each other on the hidden service, panicking, spreading rumors. Let's face it, they're essentially a bunch of pansy-assed, soft hands, office jocks with delusions of grandeur. A couple have even phoned here personally to try to speak to you. Personally. After all they have been told. It's okay, though, I took their names down and they will be disciplined.'

Jonny waved his hand dismissively. 'Yeah, I know the shit has hit the fan. But how and why and where. Talk to me, Harry.'

'Boss, the nearest I can work out is that the facility in Mexico has been breached.'

'Breached?' yelled Jonny. 'From what I heard it's been fucking leveled. By a drone strike or something.'

Harry smiled. Or to put it more accurately, Harry's lips curved up. There was no corresponding expression in his eyes. 'No, boss. Rumor. It seems as though a group of professionals attacked the place. It was obvious it was done to affect our organ donor business directly. The guards were taken out, Doctor Wegner was … well, beaten to a pulp. Literally. Someone sent pictures. I have no idea how it was done. Or why. Doors were smashed in, most probably by explosive charges. Money was stolen and the team made a clean get away. I have tried to contact the farms, including The Pastor's private cell, but to no avail. I can only assume the same, or a similar team, have taken out the supply facilities as well.'

'This is a disaster,' said Jonny. 'Who would do this? Why?'

'A couple of choices, boss,' speculated Harry. 'A rival family or faction who want to muscle in on our business. Or some group put together by a relative of someone we took for processing. To be honest, though, neither really makes sense. Plus, I have a few reports that say the attackers had a pack of trained dogs with them.'

'Dogs? That's ridiculous,' scoffed Jonny.

For the first time, Harry looked less confident than usual. 'Well, actually, boss,' he continued. 'The reports said, wolves. Big ones. And they were corroborated by a few witnesses.'

'You gotta be shitting me. So, you say we are being attacked by a bunch of wolf-wielding mercenaries who are intent on shutting down our business and we have no idea who they are?'

Harry shrugged. 'We know one of our doctors was helping them. A Miss Materia Santiago. She wasn't involved in the business, she was on the legit side. Providing cover. Witnesses saw her leave with one of the mercenaries. A big man. Very hairy. Unique looking.'

'Unique looking?' asked Jonny. 'How? What was he, a fucking hunchback or something?'

Harry looked embarrassed but didn't answer.

'Come on, Harry,' insisted Cigar Jonny. 'I know when you're holding out on me. Talk.'

'They said he looked like a wolf.'

'You mean, he wore a fur coat, that sort of thing?' asked Jonny.

The bean counter shook his head. 'No, boss. Like a wolf, but standing up. Seven-feet-high, fur, claws, big jaw full of teeth. A Wolfman.'

'*Porco Dio*,' shouted Jonny. 'God is a pig. I don't need to hear this crap, Harry. Stick to reality.'

'Yes, boss.'

'So, what now?'

'The doctors are in a flat spin, boss. They're demanding protection. Round the clock bodyguards. That sort of thing. They don't know what's going on but they're scared.'

'Can we protect them?'

Harry held his hand out in front of him and wobbled it back and forth. 'Maybe. I think what we need to ask ourselves is, do we want to?'

Cigar Jonny snorted. 'Hey, I don't like these pansy-assed doctors as much as you, but we make more money outta them than all the rest of our businesses put together.'

'Agreed, boss. But what I meant is, some of them are essential. Others, not so much. And a couple I could well see getting rid of. I made a list of three we need to keep, core members of the team. So, I recommend we put our best guys on to them. But we do it properly, move them and their families to safe houses. Keep it under the wire. We can bullshit the families that it's some sort of FBI thing. I'll run up some fake badges, ID. It'll work.

Then there's a list of four expendables. We can put the second string there, if they get made, tough, we can always replace them.

Finally, three who are shooting their mouths off, making waves. Unreliable. I say we put our worst guys with them. But we make them look like we're trying. Make a big deal out of it. Nine bodyguards each, round the clock, cars outside their houses, ostentatious, visible weapons, the whole shtick. Use them as bait. Set up a bunch of cameras around their houses. Remote surveillance. At very least we'll find out who is involved.'

Cigar Jonny chuckled. 'I can always rely on you to put things in perspective, Harry. You are one cold calculating son of a bitch.'

Harry nodded in acceptance of what he classed as a compliment. 'It's gonna leave us thin on the ground,' he warned. 'But we have enough soldiers to do it. Shall I make it so?'

'Make it so, Harry,' affirmed Cigar Jonny. 'Make it so.'

25

Houston. The largest city in Texas and the fourth largest in the United States. It contains more Fortune 500 companies than any other city. Close to the center of the town is the Texas Medical Center. The center contains over fifty medical-related institutions including twenty-one hospitals.

They do around fourteen thousand heart surgeries a year and thousands of organ transplants. A perfect place for the illegal organ industry to flourish.

There are also around three hundred murders or violent deaths a year in Houston. Brenner aimed to make a clear and obvious impact on those figures. It was time to cause a marked spike in the statistics.

Because Brenner was in the retribution business, and vengeance is oft a hard and bloody affair.

Earlier on that morning, Griff had gone onto the "Meta Global Medical Group" website and written down the address. Then he and Brenner had driven there and done what they referred to as, area reconnaissance. They merely entered the hospital and walked around, getting a feel of the place. Some would call such light recon a waste of time, but both Griff and Brenner were great believers in immersing yourself in your target. It had worked for them in Vietnam and Cambodia and they knew it would work for them now.

The hospital was your quintessential upper-income, private clinic catering for the wealthy and the fabulously wealthy, or those with the very best health insurance. A five-star hotel with doctors and nurses and machines that went beep.

But it still smelled like a hospital. A combination of surgical spirits, laundry detergent and boiled cabbage. Notwithstanding the fact that the Meta Global Hospital had never been within shouting distance of boiled cabbage. It served macrobiotic, organic haute cuisine that would grace any good restaurant. It was simply that hospitals always smelled that way. Especially to Brenner's enhanced senses.

They proceeded to the organ transplant wing, walking with a purpose so as to discourage any questions. They both knew if you walked like you knew where you were going, then people simply assumed you belonged, and they stayed out of your way.

'Lot of patients here,' noted Griff, as they walked down the corridor. 'Wonder how many of them got their organs from the Frankenstein Group?'

Brenner shrugged. 'No way to know.'

Griff sighed. 'Could be they would be dead if it wasn't for the illegal organs.'

'Yeah,' agreed Brenner. 'Doesn't make it right to kidnap and murder someone though, does it?'

Griff held a hand up. 'Preaching to the converted, Ded. Not arguing, just pointing out a fact.'

'I've seen enough,' said Brenner. 'Let's go. Time for you to do some more in-depth research.'

***

One of the patients in the ward was Rossco Johnson. And he was an alcoholic.

Hi, Rossco.

He was also a multimillionaire, having made his money the old-fashioned way. He inherited it. Rossco had no friends, but he had many acquaintances. He was fifty-four years old, and this was his second liver transplant.

Obviously, Rossco had not gone through the usual channels one goes through when applying for a liver donation. After one almost drinks oneself to death twice in a row one tends to go to the back of the queue.

But it was amazing what a million dollars will do when it comes to smoothing the road.

He knew where the organ was coming from, and he knew what he was doing was illegal. He even knew the person the liver had been stolen from had been murdered. But as Rossco so succinctly put it, 'I had a million dollars to spare, and he was just some loser with nowhere to go. Now at least some small part of him gets to live the lifestyle of the rich and famous. Well, rich, at least.'

What Rossco didn't know was the name of his unplanned benefactor. A young man who had just finished high-school and gone on a solitary road trip to find himself. Bradley Martin, high achiever, adequate sportsman, and planning to go places. Unfortunately for Bradley, he went to several different places. Rossco's liver, a middle-aged man's kidney, an elderly women's heart and, finally, a young girl's lungs.

Hayley Jackson was eleven years old and had contracted cystic fibrosis. Her only chance had been a full lung transplant. Luckily her godfather was a well-known actor who had both money and connections enough to ensure his girl got herself a new set of top-quality lungs. Courtesy of the Frankenstein Corporation and the late Master Bradley Martin.

All in all, young Bradley Martin had died, or had been murdered to be more precise, to allow four separate people to have a chance at living a life far beyond what would have been considered achievable only thirty years before. His murder had also enriched the Corporation by a little over nine hundred thousand dollars, American. A small fortune.

And he was but one in a long production line of immorality chasing immortality and enrichment.

The American dream of being able to buy life.

And the watchers watched and Brenner planned.

For justice is impartial and reasonable to the point of unreasonableness. One cannot debate with righteousness.

Brenner was going to put an end to the system and his march forward was both implacable and ruthless.

Protect the innocent weak from the evil strong.

Retribution.

26

Griff leaned back in his chair and sighed.

'What?' asked Brenner. 'They got you beat?'

The old man shook his head. 'No ways, dude. In fact, it's too easy. Well, it is, and it isn't.'

Brenner laughed. 'Well, I'm happy, and I'm sad. What do you mean?'

'I've found, maybe, ten or so doctors linked to the corporation. I say, maybe because there are three that are all over the Dark Net communications. It's like the corporation are answering every email with as much info as possible. Promising protection, giving names, times places. The whole deal.

Then there are another four dudes in the loop but not so high profile.

Finally, three doctors that were almost impossible to find. All comms with them is on the down-low. Real black ops stuff. It's like there are three separate organizations being run under the same umbrella. Doesn't make sense.'

'Could just be panic. General inefficiencies. One hand not knowing what the other hand is doing.'

'Might be,' admitted Griff. 'Tell you what, if these three groups are being run by different handlers then I propose we take on the popular dudes first. The whole setup stinks of amateur hour. Should be an in and out job, no hassles.'

'Pick one,' said Brenner. 'We'll hit them tonight.'

Griff nodded and continued his search.

***

Griff had driven them to the suburb where the target lived. They had chosen a single, male doctor. Less chance of collateral damage that way. The old man had parked the Winnebago five streets away from the doctor's residence, nestled in some trees off the road and away from any streetlights. For such a huge vehicle, Griff had done a good job blending in.

'Right,' said Brenner. 'I'll go and do a quick recce, check out guard placement and numbers.'

Griff chuckled. 'Settle, big man. Now sit back and bid welcome to the new millennium.'

'What the hell are you going on about?' questioned Brenner.

'This,' said Griff with a flourish. He produced a box, out of which he pulled a drone. 'New generation surveillance drone. Night vision, nap of the earth control, GPS, real time transmitting. It doesn't come better than this. These puppies aren't even available on the commercial market yet. Strictly law enforcement and government use only. I'll fly this dude in, it can do all the grunt work then you can take it from there.'

Brenner stared at the drone with all the inherent distrust and suspicion of a true technophobe. 'What if they hear it?' he asked.

'No ways,' argued Griff. 'It's whisper-quiet technology. Trust me, this is the way to go.'

Brenner folded his arms and said nothing.

Less than a minute later they were both looking at the target's residence in full HD color. And even Brenner had to admit he was impressed.

'Man,' he said. 'Why didn't we have these in 'Nam? Could have done with a few.'

Griff snorted. 'Dude, we were lucky they didn't make us fight with clubs and rocks. Cast your mind back, we didn't have cell phones, CD's, iPods, satnav. No body armor, Camelbak hydration packs. We had fucking boots, rifles, and napalm. Different times, man.'

'Looks like there's two guards in the vehicle parked outside. Another two patrolling the property,' noted Brenner. 'Can you look into the windows?'

'Sure,' acknowledged Griff as he piloted the drone past the lounge window.

'I guess one more inside,' continued Brenner. 'There's the doctor. Looks like he's watching TV. Drinking.'

Griff started to flick switches, sucking on his teeth as he did so.

'What's the problem?' asked Brenner.

'Getting a raft of signals coming from this place. Big time surveillance going down. I'd guess at maybe twenty cameras, all transmitting live. Infrared, sound. The whole deal. Man, someone really wants to see what's going on here. Whoever attacks this place is going to go viral. Big time.'

'You reckon they've got some serious backup just waiting around the corner? As soon as they see me they send the cavalry?'

'Why so many cameras then?' asked Griff. 'This whole thing doesn't make sense.'

'Maybe it does,' interjected Brenner.

'How?'

'Maybe this is the C team. Bait. Make a big noise to attract the predators then spring a trap. Basically, this dude is the tethered goat.'

'Could be,' admitted Griff as he piloted the drone in ever widening circles. 'Except I can't see anyone hiding near the target. If they are going to send the cavalry, then they must be encamped some distance away.'

'Maybe it's merely bait to get to see what they're up against,' ventured Brenner.

'Makes sense,' agreed Griff. 'So, what do you reckon we do?'

'We take the bait,' said Brenner. 'Is there any way you can mess with their cameras?'

'Not directly,' said Griff. 'but I can mess with the feed. Scramble the output so they go blind. As long as they don't have on-site recording facilities as well, then we're all good.'

'Do it,' instructed Brenner. 'But wait until I'm real close. Then spoil the feed. I'll be quick and quiet. Except for the doctor. I might have to have a few words with him.'

'Here,' Griff held out a small black object. 'It's an in-ear mic. You can hear me and if you speak normally, then I can hear you.'

'I'm going to go Wolfman,' warned Brenner.

'No worries,' said Griff. 'It'll stay put.'

Brenner inserted the earpiece and tapped it.

Griff nodded. 'Receiving loud and clear. Go for it. I'll keep an eye-in-the-sky on you. Then I'll cut their camera feed just before you get on site.'

The big man gave Griff a thumb up then disrobed, folding his clothes neatly over the back of the chair.

He changed as he slipped out of the Winnebago, transitioning smoothly from human to meta-human. And the human-animal hybrid vanished into the night, becoming one with the shadows and the darkness.

Brenner took out the men in the car first. As soon as Griff informed him the cameras were down he moved. Long arms reached through the open driver's window, claws grabbed heads and with a quick jerk both necks were snapped. The operation was so quiet and so quick, it seemed almost gentle. A mother lulling her children to sleep.

Forever.

Next were the two patrolling guards. They were rank amateurs. One was even smoking as he walked around the house.

The Wolfman struck. There was the gentle sound of breath being expelled. The almost imperceptible sound of a body being laid on the grass. Then nothing.

Brenner opened the back door by using his usual method

of simply turning the handle until it stripped and the door opened.

He ghosted in, turning sideways to fit through the doorway as he moved into the house.

Both the guard and the doctor saw him at the same time as he entered the sitting room. Both froze. The guard remained silent, but the doctor let out a high-pitched scream. Not loud. A steam kettle reaching the boil. Like a man in a nightmare, unable to sufficiently express the absolute terror he felt, as a creature from man's deepest darkest nightmares suddenly appeared in his home and stared at him.

The guard went for his weapon but it was too late. Brenner grabbed his head between his hands and twisted. Bone grated against bone, and the Wolfman dropped the shivering corpse to the floor before stepping over it, grabbing hold of the doctor and pulling him to his feet.

'Do you know why I am here?' asked the Wolfman.

The doctor started weeping. Loudly and with feeling. A toddler being faced with the end of the world. Mucus drained from his nose, and saliva dribbled from his loose lips as he went into absolute extremis.

'Do you know?' repeated Brenner, his words a low growl as they emanated from between his gnashing teeth.

'The organs,' whispered the doctor.

'Yes,' agreed Brenner. 'The organs of the people that were murdered.'

'I didn't know,' argued the doctor.

'Bullshit,' snapped Brenner.

'Please,' begged the doctor. 'I'm sorry. I won't do it again. Ever.'

'No, you won't,' agreed the Wolfman.

The doctor felt a thump in his lower torso, just below his navel. Then followed a pain beyond anything he had ever imagined possible. He looked down to see the creature in front of him had used one of its razor-sharp claws to eviscerate him. A deep cut ran from the doctor's navel to his breast bone.

And as he looked down, his intestines coiled out of him like a vat of escaping eels, slipping to the floor in a steaming bundle.

He tried to scream, but the agony was too great. Instead he sank slowly to the floor, clutching and pawing ineffectually at his innards, mewling and panting as he did so.

'Even this is not punishment enough,' said Brenner. 'You took an oath, and you have violated it. You are beyond evil.'

The Wolfman left the room.

As he was about to leave the house, Griff crackled in his ear. 'Hey, Ded. Got a plan. Look up, at the corner of the corridor. Can you see a small camera?'

'Brenner growled an affirmation.

'Cool. Go up to it, put your face close then growl. Don't question, just do it.'

Brenner complied, walking over to the camera, glaring at it, and peeling his lips back as he growled at it. Then he turned and left.

Less than thirty seconds later he was putting his clothes back on in the Winnebago and Griff was driving out of town.

'What the hell was that growling at the camera shit, Griff?' asked Brenner.

Griff chuckled. 'I was taking a leaf out of chief Kohana's book.'

'What?'

'Theater,' explained Griff. 'When you growled into the camera, I cleared the feed for about a tenth of a second. Just enough for them to get a blurred image of you. But not enough to be sure. Just thought I'd throw a bit of confusion into the mix. Screw with their brains a bit. As Kohana said, theater.'

Brenner laughed out loud. 'Good one, Griff. Nice.'

***

'Boss,' said Harry the bean counter. 'These guys are good. Better than anyone we've ever come across before. I mean, I'm talking government agent level. Black ops stuff. I reckon a team of at least four, maybe more. They scrambled the video and audio signals for a little under three minutes. In and out. Every bodyguard is dead. Broken necks, all of them. The two in the car hadn't even moved. The killers must have slipped into the back seat of the vehicle and taken them out together. Snap, crackle, and pop. No sign of a struggle with the other guards. One moment they were on patrol, the next, dead. Dropped where they stood. They didn't even suspect a thing.'

'And the doctor?' asked Cigar Jonny.

Harry grimaced. 'Another story. He had been eviscerated. Looks like a large scalpel or something similar. One cut from below his navel to his breastbone. Spilled his insides like a gutted farm animal. Left to die. Was still just alive when our backup team got there, but there was nothing they could do. He slipped away. Died in the most appalling agony. Kept repeating the same word over and over again. Like a mantra.'

'What?'

'Cerberus.'

'Cerberus?'

'Yep, boss. Three-headed dog, guardian to the gateway to the underworld.'

'Why?'

Harry looked embarrassed. And nervous. 'Boss, we have less than half a second of visual. It just pops on and off. You need to see it.' The bean counter fiddled with his computer and the screen flickered to life. Gray fuzz. Then a flash of … something. Harry ran his fingers over the pad, slowed the image down, rewound. They watched again.

'What the fuck is that?' gasped Cigar Jonny. 'Some sort of dog?'

'Maybe. Like some sort of hellhound,' said Harry. 'A mythical beast. Cerberus? Maybe, boss. But to me it looks more like a wolf. And a man.'

'You're not serious, Harry.'

The bean counter nodded. 'I am boss. Deadly serious. I think it's a fucking werewolf.'

27

'We need to up the game,' said Griff.

Brenner didn't react. He simply stood still, staring out across the empty scrubland they had stopped in, some twenty miles outside of Houston. He took a pack of Lucky Strikes out, lit, dragged.

'Hey, Ded. Calling all stations. You hear me?'

Brenner nodded. 'I just killed six men,' he said, his voice rough with self-recrimination. 'How do you up your game from that?'

Griff walked over and put his hand on the big man's shoulder. 'You kill ten,' he said. 'Or twenty. Or however many you need to stop this shit. They were bad people. Evil,' he continued. 'What you did was necessary. It was ordained. They transgressed, and we stopped them.'

'Who made us judge and jury?'

'We did,' answered Griff. 'We did, my man. And do you know why? Because someone has to do it. Don't you think I'd rather be sitting back, surfing the net, making just enough cash to get by, smoke, drink, and do whatever I felt like? But this shit needed to be done, Ded. Someone has to stop these assholes. And it just so happens those someones are us. So, even though we sometimes hate doing it, tough. It's what we do. And anyway, they started it by kidnapping me. Now suck it up, dude. I've got a plan. Come inside and we'll discuss it.'

Brenner finished his cigarette and flicked it out into the night. A miniature comet.

'I didn't hate killing those men,' he said to himself, his voice barely a whisper. 'I enjoyed it. And that's the problem.'

He followed his friend back into the vehicle, ready for the next part of the attack.

***

Doctor Ian Parsons was a highly successful surgeon. He was married to money, had three children, a boy and two girls, and he spent most of his waking moments feeling inadequate. Because whatever he did, however much he achieved, he would never be senator, war-hero, all-American, Randy "The Bull" Parsons.

He would never be his father.

And "The Bull" would never let him forget it. It was all very well operating on people and saving lives, his father often said, but while there are around fifteen million doctors in the world, there are only three thousand Medal of Honor recipients ever in history. Sort of humbles a man, doesn't it, he would say, with his shit-eating grin and his fake jocularity and faux humbleness.

And that was probably one of the main reasons Ian had been so open to the advance from the Corporation. Initially, they had approached him a few times, usually using women. Good-looking, earnest young women, sexy but approachable. They would talk at cocktail parties, approach him after lectures, and talk ethics, politics, and money.

After a few weeks, he was contacted by a man called Harry. Said he was an accountant for a large investment group, and he had a surefire way of quadrupling Ian's current earnings. Not only that, he would be in the position to give Ian power, prestige, and more.

Doctor Ian Parsons had jumped at the offer.

And now he worked almost exclusively for the Corporation, carrying out organ transplants using stolen organs. Using body parts that had been reaped from the unsuspecting. Literally torn from the dying bodies of innocent men, women, and children.

And with that knowledge had come a feeling of godlike power transcending all his perceived shortcomings. There may have been only three thousand Medal of Honor recipients, but there was only one Doctor Ian Parsons, a man who held the power of life and death in his very hands.

And Senator Parsons could suck it.

In fact, Doctor Ian Parsons was so important, he had his own bodyguards. Twelve of them. Four inside the house and eight patrolling the grounds. Of course, it wasn't his own house, Cigar Jonny had moved him and his family to what they called a "Safe House", as there had been threats against the Corporation. Nothing to worry about, Harry had stressed, but when you were as important to the company as Ian was then why take chances.

Why indeed?

It was late evening, and the children were asleep. His wife was also upstairs in bed. Reading most likely.

Ian sat alone in the sitting room. He had a tumbler of whisky next to him. Scotch. Single malt. On ice. Not that he was a huge fan. Truth be told, he preferred something sweeter. Sherry. Or maybe even a cocktail. But he felt a man of his standing should drink a weightier drink. And nothing was weightier than a tumbler of expensive Scotch.

He swirled the alcohol around the glass, listening to the subtle tinkle of the ice on the crystal. It was the sound of money. Of wealth. Of importance.

Then, in the background, he heard another sound. A sort of deep sigh. Strange.

'Bart,' he called out to the chief bodyguard. 'Is that you?'

No one answered.

'Bart,' he called out again.

Still nothing. Damn it. He stood and walked toward the corridor. Why wasn't Bart answering him? After all, he was, *ipso facto*, the man's boss. Goddamit, the thug worked for him. For Doctor Ian Parsons.

He was halfway across the sitting room when the creature stepped through the door.

Fully seven feet tall and so broad as to have to turn sideways to negotiate the opening. Eyes, two golden pools of horror. Teeth as long as a man's index finger. Fur, matted over slabs of muscle that looked like rough-packed concrete.

Then the creature spoke.

'Doctor Ian Parsons. You have been weighed on the scales of justice and found wanting.' And its voice was as the thunder of the heavens. The breaking of waves on jagged rock. It was the voice of the dark angel and it filled Ian with both dread and despair.

He turned to run, but it was too late.

A pair of massive clawed hands grasped his head and squeezed. With an implacable force, they ground the plates of his skull together until the internal pressure was so great the entire structure imploded, venting his brain, eyes and tongue out of its orifices and onto the floor.

Brenner dropped the body and left.

28

Griff had not disabled any of the cameras, deliberately allowing the enemy to see Brennerwolf in full HD color.

Four minutes and fifty-two seconds of unbridled violence. Harry rewound the video and pressed play again.

Once more, he and Cigar Jonny watched death unfold at a rate of one person every twenty-two seconds. The creature moved faster than both of them believed possible. A mere blur of movement in the shadows.

And this time there were no clean kills. No breaking of necks and dropping of bodies neatly where they had expired. This time the Wolfman had gone for speed. Slashing and tearing with tooth and claw. Heads rolled, limbs were scattered, and internal organs were exposed to the night air.

Where the last attack had been an exercise in stealth, this one had been a blatant show of strength.

Neither man spoke for a while.

After a few minutes, Jonny lit a fresh cigar with shaking fingers. 'That is all fucked-up,' he said. 'For the first time in my life, I truly do not know what to do.'

'You do what you always do, boss,' said Harry the bean counter. 'You fight back.'

Jonny took a deep breath. 'It's a fucking werewolf, Harry. A werewolf. You saw it, how do you fight that?'

'I'm not sure,' admitted Harry. 'With silver bullets? There

must be a way.'

'Those were some of our best men, Harry. Our best. And that thing went through them like they were kindergarten children. And why? Why is it doing this? Are we being punished by God?'

Harry snorted. 'No way, boss. If God were punishing us, do you really think he would send the Devil to do it?'

Jonny nodded. 'You're right. But look, we gotta do something and we gotta do it fast. What do you recommend?'

'We consolidate,' answered Harry. 'Bring everyone together, go to the ranch. Take all key personnel there and batten down the hatches. We got great fields of fire, the house is built like a fortress and we can see people coming from miles away.'

'How many soldiers have we got left?' asked Jonny.

'Well, we lost seventeen in the last two nights. So that leaves us with twenty-one regulars. But we can also call in the independents. That would give us another seven.'

'Do it,' instructed Jonny.

Harry spent the next twenty minutes on the phone while Jonny smoked his way through a new cigar.

Afterward the mob boss lit a fresh stogie and leaned forward in his seat. 'Harry. I've been thinking. Twenty-eight people. Even if they go on twelve-hour shifts, that's only fourteen a shift. That thing went through twelve of my best men like they weren't even there.'

'No, boss. Don't say it,' blurted Harry, his usual ice-cold

demeanor starting to crack.

'You don't know what I'm going to say,' replied Cigar Jonny. 'And remember who the boss is, Harry.'

Harry let his head droop. 'Sorry, boss.'

'I think we should give some serious thought to calling The Janitor,' continued Jonny.

'That's what I thought you were going to say, boss,' said Harry.

'And you disagree?'

'As you just said, boss, not my place to disagree. But if I may advise, he's a loose cannon. I don't trust him, and I trust his men even less. Bunch of psycho nutcases. To be perfectly honest, boss, I'm not sure who I'm more scared of, The Janitor or that Wolfman thing.'

'Well, if we're all being honest, Harry,' replied Cigar Jonny. 'I don't have that problem. I can say, without shame or embarrassment, I am more scared of that fucking werewolf. So, call The Janitor. Set up a meeting. Let's show him the recording and we'll take it from there.'

29

The man known to all as The Janitor, stood in front of the assembled men. Next to him was a sturdy wooden table laden with boxes.

As well as Cigar Jonny, the Bean Counter and The Janitor, there were another forty men present. Twenty-eight of Cigar Jonny's guns and twelve of The Janitor's soldiers.

With a quick glance, it was immediately apparent as to the difference in caliber between the two groups.

Jonny's men were street smart, armed bullyboys. Good for leaning on business men, disciplining hookers, and preying on relatively harmless shop owners. The odd bit of wet work wasn't beyond them but, as a whole, they were strong-arm men, not killers.

The Janitor's men, on the other hand, were the stuff of nightmares. Dressed in grey and black urban camo they were armed to the hilt. Assault rifles, night vision goggles, pistols, hand grenades, and combat knives.

One look at their eyes was enough to register the thousand-yard stares they all carried. The look of men who had been pushed to the limit and survived. The all-seeing gaze of the true combat veteran. Men who killed, not for pleasure, but merely because they were very good at it.

And it was all they knew how to do.

The Janitor smiled. It was a genuine sign of his enjoyment.

'Well, gentlemen,' he said. 'You've all seen the recording.' He looked around the room. Pausing. Taking in the men's expressions before he continued. 'Some serious shit, I can tell you. A fucking werewolf. Bet you never thought you would hear those words spoken for real.'

There was a murmur of agreement from Jonny's men. The Janitor's troops said nothing.

'So, our job is twofold. Protect this house and all in it. Secondly, take out the dog-man. Now, I have already instituted a plan as to how we can track down and kill the animal-man. I have tethered a goat for him. I left one of the doctors in his house with an invitation stuck to his chest.

'I figured, why track the wolf when you can simply get it to come to us. And, believe me, the son of a bitch will come. Judging from what he has done to this organization already he obviously has a real hard-on for destroying all that Mister Cigar Jonny has worked for. And he won't stop until he has reached his goal. So, he'll know it's a trap, but I reckon he won't care. He'll come anyway, full of piss and vinegar, and we'll kill him. Game over.'

Harry the Bean Counter went pale, and he leaned across to whisper into Cigar Jonny's ear. 'This is why I don't want anything to do with this psycho. He didn't even consult with us before embarking on this insane plan. Telling that wolf-thing where we are. It's gonna come here and kill us all.'

Cigar Jonny shook his head. 'I disagree. Okay, he should have asked us, but look at these men. There's no way we can fail. There are too many of us and we're just too bad. Let the animal come. We'll take him out, for sure.'

The Janitor grabbed one of the boxes stacked on the table next to him, tore it open and poured the contents out onto the tabletop.

Nine-millimeter cartridges bounced and rolled across the surface.

'Silver-plated slugs,' he said. 'Now we don't know much about werewolves but the general consensus seems to be that silver is deadly to them. It's sorta like their kryptonite. I've got enough ammo here, all calibers, to arm you all. Surprisingly, and contrary to what many people think, it's pretty easy to buy silver bullets. In fact, a lot of gun shops carry them. Must be more werewolf hunters out there than I thought.'

The Janitor laughed and there was a polite smattering of laughter in return.

'As well as this advantage, we will have a ring of EMP generators that will prevent any form of flying or electronic surveillance. Obviously, it will also negate any electronic surveillance of our own, like our CCTV cameras, but I don't see this as a problem as I will be placing more than enough sentries around the building to see anything that comes even close to us.

On top of that we are going to cover the area in good old- fashioned trip wires linked to claymore mines and flares. Trust me, gentlemen, anyone or anything tries to get inside the perimeter and we will know. And we will kill it.'

This time, instead of polite laughter, the men cheered, swept up by The Janitor's confidence and obvious professionalism.

'Come on then, men,' continued The Janitor. 'Let's get things done.'

30

'This is a trap,' said Griff.

'Probably,' agreed Brenner.

'No, not probably–definitely,' continued the old man. 'I mean, it's so obvious. The info on all the doctors goes dark except for this one. A whole bunch of emails telling him he has to wait for pickup as they can't get to him until tomorrow. It's bloody amateur hour, Ded.'

'So how many guards and stuff?' asked Brenner.

Griff shrugged. 'That's another strange thing. I've sent the drone all over the area and I can't see any sign of guards. Also, all the drapes are closed so I can't see inside the house. No sign of cameras but the lights are on. All I can surmise is that they may have rigged the place to blow. A bunch of C4 attached to a motion detector, you get inside … boom! No more Brenner.'

Brenner grinned. 'Boom?'

'Yeah, Boom!'

'I'll smell the C4 if there is any. And don't worry, I'll stay frosty. If they are trying anything funny, then I'll take care of it.'

Brenner stripped down and left the Winnebago. They had parked a couple of blocks away from the target and Brenner ghosted through the neighborhood, sticking to gardens and trees, silencing the dogs with a look or even a mere thought. Within minutes he was outside the doctor's residence.

He cased the area, sniffing at doors and windows, peeking in where possible, straining to pick up any movement inside the house.

Finally, satisfied there were no booby traps or people waiting in ambush he simply pushed hard on the back door, smashed it down and walked in. As he did, he immediately picked up another smell that hadn't been apparent from the outside. Blood.

He walked slowly through the house, checking each room as he went by. When he came to the sitting room, it was obvious where the smell of blood was coming from. Sitting on one of the wingback chairs, eyes open wide, hands by his side, was the doctor.

A large hunting knife stuck out of his chest. The knife had not only been used to kill the doctor, it had also been used as a giant tack to attach a message to the dead man's chest.

Brenner ripped the sheet of paper off and read it.

It was a map with an area circled in red and scrawled underneath the words—'Here be dragons. With love, The Janitor.'

Brenner smiled. 'Fine,' he said to himself. 'Time for some dragon slaying.'

31

Cigar Jonny chewed on his unlit cigar and kept a surreptitious eye on The Janitor. He had dealt with the mercenary before, but had spent less than a total of ten minutes in his actual company. Now, after many hours of actual face time Jonny was convinced of one thing. The Janitor was irretrievably insane.

His eyes darted from place to place, never resting and, suddenly, he would burst out laughing or, even worse, unleash a barely controlled snarl of anger. At times, he would glance into the shadows and Jonny could see a flash of real fear flitter across his face, only to be quickly replaced with anger.

Then he would laugh again.

Jonny had worked his way up through the ranks of the family by being harder than anyone else. By maintaining an aura of fear and violence around him at all times. But Jonny would have been the first to admit, if only to himself, that The Janitor scared the crap out of him.

And, as a result, he was gaining confidence this madman could defeat the Wolfman who was coming to kill him. He knew it meant that he would owe The Janitor. Big time. But that was then, and this was now. And now was all that worried Cigar Jonny at the moment.

The Janitor laughed again.

***

'Bastards fried my drone,' shouted Griff as he slammed his fist against the screen.

'How?' asked Brenner.

'Not sure,' admitted the old man. 'Most likely some sort of industrial strength EMP emitter. Must be real heavy duty because the drone is shielded against shit like that. Assholes.'

'So, I'll be going in blind,' stated Brenner.

'Yep. It's the old-fashioned way from here on in.'

Brenner grimaced. 'This place has been well-chosen. No high points for any sniper overwatch, no vegetation for at least a mile around. It's gonna be tough.'

'Also, no in-ear comms,' added Griff. 'Their EMP will screw it up. So, you're properly on your own.'

'Be just like the old days,' said Brenner as he stripped down.

Griff watched him as he went full wolf and drifted off into the night.

Brenner loped through the sparse brush, keeping low and following the natural folds in the ground. Blending with the shadows, moving fast but not sprinting.

In less than two minutes he was at the perimeter of the ranch house. There was no fence as such but the earth had been cleared in a full circle and, even though great care had been taken to conceal them, Brenner immediately saw at least three dug in guard emplacements.

The massive wolf went to ground, slinking along on its belly. A mere shadow amongst shadows. There but not there.

He crawled toward the first emplacement, his movements as slow as cancer. And as insidious. All senses on high alert.

He saw the trip wire with ease. In fact, he would have known it was there even with his eyes closed. It stank of man-sweat, tobacco, and gun oil. With great care, he skirted around it then readjusted his heading back to the guard's location.

He stopped some twenty yards away and watched. It was immediately apparent to him that these were not the same caliber of men he had come up against at the other doctor's residences. These were not mere street thugs and gangsters. They were men like him. Most likely ex-military. Probably special forces.

Killers.

Brenner lay still and watched. In his head, his internal clock ticked on, slicing off little moments of life and casting them away as the hour slipped by.

He sensed someone approach. Moving stealthily but surely. Two more guards arrived. There was a brief discussion, and they changed places.

Brenner grinned a wolfy grin to himself. They had changed on the hour. Exactly. So, they weren't as professional as they thought they were. A true pro would never change guard on the hour, letting the clock dictate his agenda. Change of shift should always be random.

Seventeen minutes past, or fourteen minutes to.

Never at the top of the hour as it allows the enemy to plan, to predict. Just as Brenner was now doing.

The wolf waited for another twelve minutes then he started to edge forward. Slowly. Carefully. Until he was mere feet away from the lip of the trench housing the two guards.

He leapt.

They died.

The shadow slid from the foxhole and headed for the next brace of guards. Moving with confidence and treating the ill-disguised tripwires with disdain.

Mere minutes later the next two guards were dispatched. Then the next.

As Brenner launched himself into the trench housing the fourth pair of guards, the side of the dugout collapsed and Brenner had to twist hard to realign his attack. It was important both guards were dispatched within seconds and that both kills were performed by tearing out their throats and preventing any calls for help or cries of alarm.

Four more guards died in the next twenty minutes. Brenner trading stealth for speed.

He was lucky in that the last two foxholes contained men similar to the ones he had come up against before. Street thugs who were totally out of their comfort zone. In fact, they were so bad that the last pair were even smoking and chatting like they were at some sort of social gathering.

They died like the others, their lack of professionalism

ultimately making no difference to their end fate.

Then he was outside the ranch house itself. He morphed into his Wolfman mode, standing seven feet tall, muscles packed upon muscles. Eyes glowing golden in the dark. Claws like garden shears and teeth like combat knives.

It was time.

Bad things were about to start happening to bad people.

32

The ranch house was a large, block-like building. It was built around a central courtyard, three stories high, crenulations on the roof and small exterior windows. Much like a miniature medieval castle.

Brenner could see at least four gunmen on the roof. They had not spotted him yet.

But they soon would.

He took a deep breath then simply ran toward the building and jumped, scaling the forty-foot wall in one mighty leap.

As he landed on the roof, his surprise advantage ceased. Shots rang out and warnings were shouted as the men reacted to the sudden presence of a seven-foot-tall monster appearing before them like magic.

Brenner moved constantly, knowing that a moving target is infinitely more difficult to hit than a static one. Two of the roof guards were soldiers, the other two were street thugs. The thugs went first, their movements slow and sluggish. Their combat awareness almost non-existent.

The two soldiers were slightly more of a challenge. They had split up and were both taking controlled and aimed shots. Their only problem was they were working at human speed whereas Brenner was working at superhuman speed.

Not one shot got within six feet of him.

With another four down, Brenner kicked the roof door in

and proceeded down to the top floor. It was a simple design. Horseshoe shaped with a screening wall covering the open end of the horseshoe so the only way in was via a massive, steel-bound front door. The top floor consisted of a corridor with all the rooms leading off the one side, facing the courtyard.

Brenner started his search by simply smashing through the first door and checking the room.

Empty.

After that, he employed a method of room-to-room that had been perfected by the Israelis. They call it walking-through-walls. It basically assumes one no longer sees a building or environment as a standard structure where your movement is dictated by set doors and windows. One simply uses explosives to create your own ingress points.

In Brenner's case, he did it without explosives. He literally, walked-through-walls.

And if you are in a room waiting for someone to come through the door and suddenly a seven-foot Wolfman comes crashing through the wall ... well ... let's just say you will find yourself at a distinct tactical disadvantage.

Terminally so.

***

Cigar Jonny bit through his cigar and let out an involuntary yelp as the sounds of upstairs walls being demolished shook the building.

'What the hell is going on up there?' shouted the Bean Counter.

The Janitor laughed out loud and clapped his hands together. 'Man, that thing is good,' he exclaimed. 'He got through the sentries and the tripwires like they weren't even there. Awesome.'

'Well are the sentries going to come and help?' asked Jonny.

The Janitor laughed again. Genuine amusement. 'Don't be stupid, Cigar,' he said, his voice full of scorn. 'They're all dead for sure. A predator like that doesn't make the rookie error of leaving potential enemies alive. But he's shown his hand and there are more than enough of us to finish him off.' He adjusted his webbing, checked his pistol, and drew a ten-inch blade Bowie knife. 'It's time to die, dog-boy,' he whispered, almost to himself.

And Cigar Jonny looked at The Janitor and shivered, convinced he could see his eyes shining with an internal fire.

Ethereal.

Otherworldly.

Demon-fire.

33

Brenner stood tall amongst the rubble from the wall he had just smashed through.

In front of him was a family.

Two children, a boy and a girl. The male, perhaps eleven or so. The girl younger. Seven, maybe eight. The mother stood in front of them, her arms held out protectively, her face a mixture of fear and anger.

In front of them all, on his knees and shivering in terror, was the father. Brenner recognized him straight away from the mug shots Griff had shown him.

Doctor Neil Ramsgate.

'What are you?' asked the mother.

'I am retribution,' growled the Wolfman.

'Well, we have done nothing wrong,' stated the woman. 'Leave us. Leave my family. We won't be any trouble.'

Brenner shook his head and pointed at the doctor. 'I am here as a direct result of your husband's actions,' said Brenner.

'What actions?'

'Don't listen to him,' yelled the doctor, his voice high-pitched. Shrill with terror as tears ran down his face. 'Leave us alone,' he sniveled.

'He is a murderer,' said Brenner. 'He is part of a ring that kidnaps innocents and kills them to harvest their organs.'

'Neil, is this true?'

'I help people, Sheila. I help sick people to live full lives. I don't know what he's talking about. I ... God, what the hell is going on? How did this happen? They said we would be safe. They promised.' He looked up at Brenner. 'I did it for the better good.'

'You all say that,' answered Brenner.

The mother started to cry. Softly. 'Please, sir, leave him. For the children's sake. Leave their father. Let him live.'

'If only he had given his victims' families that choice,' said Brenner as he shook his head. He held out his clawed hand to the doctor. 'Come with me. Stop sniveling, man. Let your children remember you as a man of strength.'

The doctor tried to pull himself together but he couldn't. His fear overcame him and he burst into tears, sniffing, and blubbering like a toddler. Brenner grasped his wrist and pulled him to his feet.

'You made my daddy cry,' said the young girl accusingly.

Brenner nodded. 'I know. I am sorry, little one.'

And Brenner smashed through the opposite wall into the next room. It was empty. Without further ado, the Wolfman tore the doctor's head from his body and tossed the two separate parts out of the window before his family could see the remains of their father and husband.

A necessary reckoning had taken place.

He plowed through to the next room to surprise two of the street thugs. They were guarding another three doctors. All of them simply stared, open-mouthed at him as he appeared. Two quick swipes of his claws and the disemboweled thugs fell to the floor, twitching in their death throes.

Brenner herded the doctors into the corner.

'Do you know why I am here?' he asked.

The one answered. 'The organ harvesting.'

'Correct,' affirmed Brenner.

The doctor nodded. 'It was wrong. Any chance of forgiveness?'

Brenner shook his head. 'No. But I will make it quick.'

'Make what quick?' screamed another one of the doctors. 'What the fuck is this freak talking about. Where are the rest of the guards? Where is Mister Jonny? Where is ...'

'Shut up, Donald,' said the first doctor. 'It's over. We transgressed. We broke our oaths. We deserve whatever we get.'

He turned to face Brenner and closed his eyes.

The Wolfman struck.

The three doctors died in a welter of blood.

Justice.

There were no more rooms left on the top floor.

Brenner kicked the last door open and jumped to the next level, eschewing the stairs.

***

'Man, listen, he's smashing through the walls to go room-to-room,' said The Janitor. 'Standard Israeli protocol except he's doing it by hand instead of using explosives.' He laughed. 'This thing is awesome. I mean, I haven't had so much fun since … well, since forever, it seems.'

'He's killing everyone,' yelled Jonny.

'Yeah,' agreed The Janitor. 'I must admit, I totally underestimated this one. Hoowee, I'm gonna mount his fucking head on my wall. Gonna make a fine trophy. Might even add his wolf-ears to my gook ear-necklace. Mighty fine.'

'You're insane,' said Jonny.

'Yeah, well, fuck you,' retorted The Janitor. 'At least I ain't a fat shit in a badly tailored suit. Now shut up and let me concentrate.'

34

The third room on the second floor revealed two more doctors. There were no guards and Brenner suspected he had gone through them all by now.

However, the one doctor had a snub nose .38 and, to be fair, his reaction times were faster than any of the professionals Brenner had so far encountered.

He blasted off a couple of rounds, one of which struck Brenner in the chest, the underpowered slug barely penetrating the super-dense muscle.

The Wolfman nodded in approval. 'Well done,' he growled. 'Good response times. Fast. Now, it's time to pay the piper, gentlemen. An eye for an eye and all that crap.' He punched into their chests, using both hands at once to rip out their hearts.

Holding them up above him he threw his head back and howled. The building itself shook as the atavistic call cut through all around, declaiming its power. Announcing its authority.

There was no one else on the second floor and as Brenner sprung over the landing to land on the first floor he knew it was near the endgame.

He was busy contemplating the various doorways, wondering which one he should enter first when he heard a voice calling out for him.

'Hey dog-boy. We're in the room at the end of the

corridor. Hurry now, don't make me come out there and fetch you.'

Brenner walked down the corridor and stood next to the door, taking care not to stand directly in front of it in case someone decided to open up with an assault rifle or similar. After a few seconds, he reckoned to take the direct route and he launched himself at the door, crashing through it and rolling right before springing to his feet.

There were three men in the room. Two dressed in suits, sitting on a sofa and the third, standing, in full combat gear. Urban camo, body armor, a Colt 45 and a large Bowie in a chest sheath.

The man in the combat uniform nodded a greeting. 'Hi,' he said as he pointed at the two men sitting behind him. 'These two are, Jonny, he's the fat one, and his accountant, whose name I forget right now. I am The Janitor, capital T, capital J. And you would be?'

'I would be your death,' said Brenner.

The Janitor laughed. 'Good one, except I don't think so.' He started to move, bringing his Colt into line as he took a step to the side.

And Brenner froze as he looked into The Janitor's eyes. Just for a microsecond. An infinitesimal amount of time. Because what he saw there was pure evil, the likes of which he had never come across before. And it chilled him to the bone.

The Janitor pulled the trigger, burning off all eight rounds in under a second.

Two of the rounds struck Brenner. The one punching into the meat of his right shoulder and the second causing a deep graze on the right side of his torso.

'Ha,' shouted The Janitor. 'Got you. Silver bullets. You're done for now, devil spawn.'

Brenner grunted in pain as the slug in his shoulder was expelled and the wound stared to heal. 'Who the hell do you think you are, the Lone Ranger?' he laughed. 'Silver bullets my ass.'

'Oh, shit we're all gonna die,' screeched Jonny.

'Shut up, Sausage,' commanded The Janitor. 'It ain't over till it's over and I haven't even begun to fight.' He squinted at Brenner. 'So, silver don't do shit?'

The Wolfman nodded. 'Maybe if I was a werewolf, but I'm not. I'm a failed US Army experiment. Nothing supernatural about me.'

'Really?'

'Yep.'

The Janitor laughed. 'And you really believe that? What an asshole.'

The Janitor drew his Bowie and the two of them circled each other for a few seconds, looking for a gap. Then Brenner struck. But The Janitor parried his claws with the Bowie and moved out of the way with comparative ease. Brenner was impressed. And puzzled. The Janitor was almost as fast as he was. In fact, if he was to be perfectly honest, there was every chance the man in front of him was actually faster than him.

They clashed again and this time The Janitor managed to break through Brenner's guard, slashing him across the chest. The wound was shallow and healed up almost immediately, but Brenner was concerned that it had happened at all.

'What are you?' he asked

The Janitor shook his head. 'Not sure, to tell the truth. Always been the fastest and the strongest. The best. Ever since Korea.'

'You fought in Korea? That was over sixty-five years ago.'

'Yep,' agreed The Janitor, as he kept circling. 'And you?'

'Vietnam. Rangers.'

'Rangers are shit.'

'Fuck you,' countered Brenner.

Before they could re-engage the sound of a gunshot thumped through the room and a slug buzzed past Brenner's head and struck the wall. The two combatants turned to see the Bean Counter standing up, his revolver in hand as he tried to draw a bead on the Wolfman.

The Janitor held up his hand. 'I swear to God,' he said. 'If you don't put that weapon down right now I will kill you myself. And it will be slow and painful. Now sit down and shut up.' He turned back to Brenner. 'Sorry about that. No sense of occasion. Asshole.'

The two of them blurred into motion once again, claw striking blade as they jockeyed for position.

Then The Janitor faked right. And Brenner fell for it.

The ten-inch Bowie entered the Wolfman's belly, low and

to the right, driving in at least three inches.

But instead of pulling back as any normal creature would have done, Brenner stepped forward, allowing the blade to penetrate even deeper, trapping it there in a grip of iron hard muscle.

He grabbed The Janitor's head between his clawed hands.

The Janitor smiled. 'Brilliant,' he said. 'I didn't see that one coming.'

Brenner snapped his neck and let the body fall to the floor. Then he pulled the Bowie knife from his belly and held it loosely in his right hand.

He turned to face the two remaining men in the room, breathing deeply and slowly to control the pain from his wound. Waiting for his power to heal him.

'How much?' asked the Bean Counter. 'We are a very cash-rich organization and every man has his price. One, two, three million?'

'I don't deal with dead men,' answered Brenner as he flicked the Bowie underhand. The ten-inch blade thudded into the Bean Counter's forehead, penetrating his skull completely as the tip of the blade emerged from the back of his cranium.

His body slid slowly off the sofa and flopped to the floor, his face etched with an expression of almost comical surprise.

Jonny drew his cigar case from his jacket pocket. He opened it and offered Brenner. The Wolfman shook his head.

'Do you mind?' asked the gangster.

'Go ahead.'

With shaking hand Jonny clipped the end from a cigar, lit it and puffed it to life.

'How many people died for your organ business?' asked Brenner.

Jonny shrugged. 'I don't know. At a guess, maybe a hundred. Maybe double that. Maybe more.' He pointed at the dead man with the Bowie knife in his head. 'He would have known. Not me.'

'Every one of those people had families,' said Brenner. 'Mothers, fathers, sons, and daughters. Your murder factory affected the lives of thousands of innocent people. Thousands.'

Jonny shrugged again, but said nothing.

Brenner lashed out. His claws struck Jonny in the face, tearing off the flesh and shattering the bone. The gangster fell to the floor, writhing in absolute agony, his screams dulled by the fact his jaw had been smashed into a hundred shards of bone.

Brenner watched him impassionedly for almost a minute. Then he struck again, his claws tearing the man's face clean off the bone like a fillet of fish.

Satisfied justice had taken place; he turned and left the room.

As he walked past the body of The Janitor he wondered again what he was. How had he lived so long? Why was he so fast? And strong? Was he also a part of the Bloodborn

Project? Or were there more black op research projects he had never heard of. More conspiracies.

Or was it deeper than that.

Something arcane.

Unfathomable.

Supernatural.

As always, the room was dark. Vertical blinds covered the single window, blocking out the sun. A large desk stood in the middle. Behind it, a well-worn leather chair. In front, two more chairs, newer but of vastly inferior quality. Government Issue. The desk itself was old. Not antique, simply old. Shabby. But like the leather chair, it was solidly built. Quality workmanship.

The colonel sat in the comfortable old leather chair, his hands steepled in front of him. Head cocked to one side. Thinking. He took a sip of tea from a china cup and replaced it delicately on its saucer.

In the corner of the room stood another man. And although he was monstrous he seemed almost made up of shadow. There, but not there. You had to look closely to register that he was present.

There was a knock on the door. The colonel stood, walked over to the blinds, and twisted the pull slightly, opening it up so a blade of light cut into the room.

He knew he was being childish and petty, but he didn't care.

Then he returned to his chair, sat, and pushed a button on the underside of the desk. The door buzzed open.

Another man walked in. Dressed in a black suit, black shirt, black boots. On his hands, black gloves crafted from the finest kidskin, almost as thin as latex. A black Trilby hat.

Aviator sunglasses. Around his neck, a black silk neckerchief. Skin as pale as a shroud.

He strode across the room, carefully avoiding the slice of sunlight lying across the floor like a tripwire. His movements were beyond graceful. Liquid smooth. His footsteps soundless on the cheap nylon carpeting. He sat on one of the inferior chairs.

'West,' said the colonel. 'Houston. Lot of dead bodies. Torn to pieces. The locals have it down as a pack of dogs, maybe a bear.'

'It's him?' asked the man in black.

'I think so,' replied the colonel. 'Too messy to be anyone else. Also, someone riding a crappy old rat bike has been seen in the area. That same someone is hanging out with an old man in a Winnebago.'

'That would be Griff,' said the man in black. 'I'll set off as soon as the sun goes down.'

'Good. This time I want you to take Lenny. You could do with a bit of extra muscle.'

'I work alone,' said the man in black. 'Well, with Howard, of course.'

'Yes you do,' agreed the colonel. 'But the thing is, you haven't actually achieved much of late. You will take Lenny. And this time you will find Brenner and bring him back. His presence is essential to the project. Don't fail me again, Sergeant Solomon. Lenny, go with the sergeant.'

The massive man stepped forward and walked over to the table, shaking the floorboards with every step.

Solomon glanced up at him. Six feet seven high, probably four hundred fifty pounds plus. Arms disproportionally long with hands like wheelbarrows. His head was square-shaped with a broad forehead and large red lips. Tiny ears and eyes set close together. He was profoundly ugly. People had nicknamed him The Troll. But they never called him that to his face. Ever.

As he walked forward the desk shuddered and the tea cup and saucer balanced on the edge slipped off.

Lenny moved forward, grabbing it before it hit the floor. The speed at which he moved was eye-watering.

Carefully, he replaced the set on the desk. Unfortunately he had totally crushed it, and all that remained was a fine ceramic powder.

He grinned, pleased he had averted an accident.

Solomon rolled his eyes. 'Great,' he exclaimed. 'Now I have to work with a cross between a human being and a bulldozer. Fucking moron.'

Lenny looked upset as he stared at the powder on the desk, finally realizing that not all had gone according to plan.

'Whatever,' said the colonel. 'Find Brenner and bring him back.'

Solomon shook his head. 'Yeah, come on Lenny. Let's go find the Wolfman.'

The man in black left without saying goodbye, and the ambulatory mountain trundled after him. Like an M1 Abrams main battle tank.

It was time to bring Brenner back into the fold.

FROM THE AUTHOR

Thanks for reading the second Bloodborn book. I hope you enjoyed it. Please check out the next one as we follow Brenner deep into the rabbit hole of reality. Things are about to get weird ... I just hope our favorite werewolf—sorry, failed US army experiment—can take it.

Once again—if you enjoyed the book (or even if you didn't) please could you leave a review. I know it's a hassle but us indie authors really do rely on your generosity.

If you would like a chat or would like to leave me some advice. My personal email is zuffs@sky.com drop me a line and I will get back to you straight away.

Thanks again—your friend, Craig.

Made in the USA
Middletown, DE
26 October 2023